Young Love and Tragedy

The Felton Chronicles

by

Mary Duncan

Published by
Brighton Publishing LLC
501 W. Ray Rd.
Suite 4
Chandler, AZ 85225

Young Love and Tragedy

The Felton Chronicles

by

Mary Duncan

Published by
Brighton Publishing LLC
501 W. Ray Rd.
Suite 4
Chandler, AZ 85225
brightonpublishing.com

First Edition

Copyright © 2012

ISBN 13: 978-1-936587-71-1

ISBN 10: 1-936-58771-8

Cover Design by: Tom Rodriguez

Chapter One

*T*ara Jackson and Megan Keys were raised together in the small town of Felton, Georgia. They were the same age and they shared everything including their birthday. They were very close friends. Although they were not sisters, people often thought they were because they were so close.

The girls' mothers were also very close friends, and had been since high school. Angela Jackson and Kinsley Keys were also inseparable as young girls. It never failed, when you saw one of them the other wasn't but a few steps behind. They even shared the same classes together in school, ensuring them less time apart.

Angela Jackson was the captain of the high school cheer leading squad and needless to say she was very popular and very well liked. Her husband Dave was the football team quarter back. He was also popular and well liked. Angela and Dave made the perfect couple. They were still very much in love with each other even after all of these years.

They had one other child besides Tara and that was her older brother James. He was following in his father's footsteps with the whole football fascination. However, Dave chose a different path once he entered college. He decided he wanted to become a homicide detective, which is what he is today. James, on the other hand, decided he wanted to go to West Georgia College on a football scholarship in hopes of going pro.

Angela Jackson had always expressed an admiration for fashion design, even from the time she was a young girl; and of course it came as no surprise when she chose that field for a career. She opened a shop in Carrolton and had been doing quite well for herself. She was extremely talented in fashion and often designed uniforms for the cheerleading squad.

Tara, like her mother was also the cheerleading captain for her high school squad. She loved the attention she received from everyone. Angela got a thrill out of her daughter's choice to mimic her high school experience as captain of the cheerleading team. Tara spent a great deal of time practicing new routines for the squad, and had an extraordinary knack for cheerleading. It just seemed to come natural for her. Her younger years in gymnastics were a significant contributing factor to her athletic ability.

Megan was the co-captain of the cheerleading squad and would spend many long hours with Tara, working together on new material for the team. Megan and James had become quite an item in the previous six months. Megan always adored James, but he was a couple of years older than her and just recently started to look at her in the same way. She was a sophomore and he was a senior.

Tara was dating a football player, too. His name was Jake Lawson. He and James were good friends as well, and much like Tara and Megan, they had been for many years. At first James wasn't too fond of his best friend dating his little sister, but after a short while he was okay with it.

Tara's and Megan's schedule was very much the same, except for the occasional time alone with the boyfriends, and most of the time they would all just hang out together. They became known as the fantastic foursome at

2

school. All four of the kids were admired by their classmates and teachers alike.

Megan's mother, Kinsley, unfortunately had not shared the same kind of luck as her good friend Angela. Kinsley was a single parent as her husband, Jason, was killed in the line of duty.

Jason and Dave were partners. They received a call one night to a location where there were reports of gunfire coming from a residence. The two officers cautiously approached the home. Dave was guarding the front door and Jason was guarding the back door. Dave knocked on the door, but there was no response. Unexpectedly, the suspect bolted out the back door with his weapon drawn and fired at Jason striking him in the left side of his chest. The bullet penetrated his heart killing him instantly.

Dave still carries around lingering feelings of guilt about Jason's death. He and Jason were great friends for many years and he thought of him as a brother. It was hard for him to accept the fact that his life must go on without Jason, and even harder to realize there was nothing he could have done any differently to prevent his death.

Megan was born two weeks after Jason was killed. He never knew the joy of meeting his daughter, nor did she ever know the joy of having a father in her life. Megan had almost come to look at Dave as a dad because he was so good to her, and always watched out for her and her mother.

Kinsley never married again. She just devoted her time and love to her little girl and her career. She was a healthcare manager at a local medical center. She made a handsome sum of money which allowed her to comfortably care for her and Megan. She was very thankful for her baby girl and the two of them were very close. Megan was much like her father, and she kept his memory very much alive for Kinsley. She couldn't imagine a life without her.

Kinsley relied on her mom and dad for emotional support after Jason's death. They were extremely helpful in every facet of her life and helped her a great deal. She lived with them for a while after Jason was killed. Karen, Kinsley's mother, was very helpful in the caretaking of her granddaughter. She often kept Megan, allowing Kinsley the security and comfort of working without having to worry about her daughter's well-being.

Unfortunately Kinsley's mother and father were killed in a car accident when Megan was five, creating yet more heartache for Kinsley to overcome. She loved her parents very much and it took some time to find a level of normalcy in her everyday life. The only thing that allowed her to go on was her love for her daughter. She knew she had to continue to push forward for her. Megan also took her grandparents death exceptionally hard, since they had been such an important part of her life. Every memory she could recall up until that time, included her grandma and grandpa, and she missed them very much.

Several years earlier, Angela and Kinsley managed to find and purchase two houses directly across the street from each other. This way they would be close and could help each other with the kids also. If one of the women had to work, the other could keep an eye on the children. Angela worked first shift and Kinsley worked second shift which was very convenient. Their children were old enough to stay home alone now, but Angela and Kinsley still felt more comfortable knowing someone was always there if something happened.

It was October and school was scheduled to get out the following May. That meant James would be leaving for West Georgia College in a few months. He would be staying in a dorm on the premises. Megan was proud of him for his achievement, and that he was going to college, but at the same time she was very upset about him leaving. She loved him and didn't want to be away from him.

The Polk County fair was in town this week and it was Friday night, so Tara, Megan, James, and Jake made plans to go together. They loved to ride the rides and play the games, not to mention hanging out with some of their other friends from school. Their parents made an exception and extended their curfew to one in the morning, allowing them time to grab a bite to eat afterwards.

James was pressuring Megan lately about having sex and she held up without caving in thus far. She didn't know how much longer she would be able to hold out. Her mother started her on birth control two years ago, but until now Megan hadn't felt the need to rely on them. She was still a virgin. She was scared of upsetting her future with a pregnancy, and she knew there was always that possibility even if she used protection. She loved James and couldn't stand the thought of losing him over this. She hadn't said anything to Tara because she didn't want James to get mad at her, knowing that Tara would probably say something to him if she knew what was going on with him.

Megan felt very alone facing two extreme fears and not knowing how to deal with them. One was becoming pregnant, and the other was losing her boyfriend. She weighed the possibility that she might not end up pregnant and if she didn't, it would solve her problem. She also wanted James to be her first, and hopefully her last. She had already entertained the prospect of becoming Mrs. James Jackson. She couldn't help but wonder how their lives would change once he went off to college and started to meet other girls. She wasn't sure he loved her as much as she loved him. Just then Megan's train of thought was broken by the sound of the phone.

"Hey girl what's up?" Tara asked.

"Excited about the fair tonight; how about you?" Megan asked.

"You know I am! Can I borrow a shirt from you? I need a blue one."

"Sure, you know you can. Come over and get it. What time are we supposed to leave?"

"We are leaving at seven o'clock. You guys are riding with us, right?" Tara asked.

"As far as I know we are. I'll see you in a minute. I am about to take a shower."

Megan grabbed a towel and left for the shower. She wasn't worried about Tara being able to get in when she locked the door, because Tara had a key. She would figure out what she was going to wear once she showered. All she could think about was James and their circumstances, and she was so confused. She for sure couldn't speak to her mom about this, as she would absolutely have a fit. She simply had to solve this one on her own and it definitely wasn't going to be easy to do.

By the time Megan finished, Tara had already let herself in and was in the closet looking for something to wear. She couldn't decide between two very similar shirts and she asked Megan which one would be best. Megan just pointed at one and Tara put it on. They both would have looked equally good on her.

Following the dilemma of the shirts, there was the difference in the shade of eye shadows to wear, and then of course, it was what accessories would best finish off the wardrobe. After they finally made their choices they grabbed their purses and headed out the door. They were going back to Tara's house to wait for James and Jake.

"Hello," Tara answered.

It was James. He decided that he and Megan were going to take his car tonight, instead of riding along with Tara and Jake. He wanted to spend some time alone with Megan.

"Okay big brother, no problem. I'll tell her. Love you!" Tara said.

"That was James, Tara explained to Megan. He said you guys are going in his car tonight. He said he wants some time alone with you. He'll be here in about ten minutes. Jake is bringing him."

"We haven't been spending much time alone lately and neither have you and Jake. I'm sure you two could use some time alone too, huh? We're still going to hang together at the fair aren't we? I hope so," Megan expressed.

A few short moments later a car drove into the driveway. It was James and Jake. The girls got into separate cars with their boyfriends and they began their journey to the fair. They would wait for each other at the front entrance gate when they got there. They would all get arm bands so they could ride every ride as many times as they wished.

Chapter Two

*I*n the distance, the sky was lit up from the fair so bright it almost looked like it was daylight. The closer James and Megan got to the fairgrounds the more congested the traffic became. There was no doubt that it was going to be hard to find a parking place close to the front entrance gate. They were hoping they would be lucky anyway and find one somewhere close.

After waiting fifteen minutes to get in the gate, James and Megan were finally directed to the third row from the back for parking. They spotted Tara and Jake's car one row up. At least James and Megan knew Tara and Jake would be at the entrance gate waiting for them. This would save them the time of running around trying to find them.

Just then, Megan heard someone calling her name from the crowd. When she looked she realized it was Tara. She and Jake were standing by the merry go 'round waiting for them. They were surrounded by a crowd of kids from school. Megan and James went to join their click.

"Hey, you guys, are ya'll ready to go ride or do you want to do some games first?" Tara asked.

"Let's go ride some rides first. I hear they have a new roller coaster called the Jumble Jack. Let's see if we can find it," Megan said.

The kids were off in search of the new ride with anticipation. It was the first roller coaster the small fair ever owned that went upside down. Most of the rides were the same year after year. It was about time they decided to add a new one.

At the roller coaster, their friends Tabitha and Randy got in one seat together and Grace and Tank got in the seat behind them. Tara and Jake would be next, and James and Megan would be last. Once they were all seated and the bars were locked in place, the operator started the ride. They started out slow, and then all of a sudden the roller coaster picked up speed. Before they knew it they were travelling at a very high rate of speed, and then hanging upside down. Everyone was screaming and shouting.

The kids weren't prepared for the next thing that would take place. With no thought of danger at all they were enjoying the excitement of the adrenalin rush, when one of the seats unattached itself from the coaster and flew through the air. Everyone was shocked at what they just witnessed. Were they mistaken? This had never happened at the county fair before.

"Oh my God, did you see that? That ride just sailed off of the track! I can't believe it!" Tara shouted hysterically.

As the horror began to sink in, they realized one of the cars flew through the air and landed in the crowd. It was the one Tabitha and Randy were sitting in. The operator was rotating the ride back to its starting place where he could get the remaining people off of it. The kids immediately ran to check on their friends to see if they were okay.

When they reached the car, they were even more horrified at the sight before them. Randy and Tabitha were both unconscious and covered with blood. Emergency medical services were on their way, but judging from what the kids saw, there would be little they could do to help them. Tara decided to call Tabitha's mother and let her know that her daughter was involved in an accident. She asked James to call Randy's parents and let them know also.

"Is this Mrs. Sealy?" Tara asked.

"Yes it is. Can I help you?

"Mrs. Sealy, there has been an accident here at the fair and Tabitha was involved in it. It's real bad and you probably need to come down here as soon as you possibly can."

"What happened? Is she okay? Is my little girl okay? Who is this anyway?" Jane Sealy exclaimed.

Tara explained to her the circumstances of the accident and Mrs. Sealy was very upset. She told Tara she was on her way. Tara said she would inform the emergency workers she would be there very shortly. James also informed Randy's parents of the urgent situation with their son. They too were on their way.

Everyone was surrounding the accident site and the emergency personnel were starting to arrive. They had to clear the people out of the way, so they could get to the kids and assess the extent of their injuries.

As the rescue staff approached Randy and Tabitha, they immediately attempted to resuscitate them. They immediately searched for their pulse and heartbeat. The injuries sustained to the teenage bodies were extremely severe. They soon discovered Tabitha was already expired, probably on impact, and they covered her with a sheet. Randy was still barely alive.

Jane Sealy and her husband Bill were the first parents to arrive at the scene. They made their way to the destructive panorama in search of their daughter. They were grief stricken with terror when they discovered the sight of Tabitha's lifeless body covered with a sheet. They knew right away what this meant, and so did everyone else gathered around them.

"Oh no, my baby, she has to be okay! Uncover my daughter, she's not dead! She has to be okay! Uncover her right now and I mean it! I want to take her home!" Jane screamed in anguish.

Bill grabbed his wife and held her tightly trying desperately to console her, even though his heart was breaking in two. He knew his wife needed him to be strong for her, and it took all the strength he could muster to hold her back. He was trying his best to get her out of there. He needed to find out which hospital they would be taking Tabitha's body to. Just as he turned to take Jane to the car she collapsed.

"Help me please! My wife just fainted. Somebody help me please!" he called out.

One of the paramedics rushed over to check on Jane and decided to put her into an ambulance. It was obvious she was overwhelmed and shocked at the realization her daughter had died.

"We are taking your wife to Polk Medical Center. That is where we will be taking your daughter as well. We will have someone notify you when we get her there. The hospital will need to talk to you in order to make arrangements for your daughter's body. We will also need you to make a definite identification on your daughter, sir. I'm very sorry for your loss," the paramedic expressed.

Bill climbed up in the back of the ambulance with Jane. He couldn't believe the turn of events that had taken place today. What started out as a normal day turned out to be the most horrifying day he had ever experienced. He started to run through the whole spectrum of what if's in his mind. What if they hadn't let Tabitha go to the fair tonight, would she still be alive? What if they had gone with her? What if they had told her not to ride the new ride? Although there was nothing that he or his wife could have done to prevent this from happening, they would always wonder, what if they had done something differently, would their daughter still be alive?

Bill was overcome with the thought that his little girl would never be coming home. She was so cheerful and caring and was very popular and seemed to be well-liked by everyone who knew her. Tabitha had a very open and outgoing personality and could brighten your day with her very presence. She was a very positive person in any situation.

The thought suddenly entered Bill's mind that Tabitha's boyfriend Randy was also in critical condition and might die as well. Randy had been Tabitha's boyfriend since they were in the fourth grade. They just became engaged a month ago. They were scheduled to graduate in May and were going to be married in August. How could this happen? They were such good kids. They were destined to be together, but now they may die together instead. This seemed so unfair. If Randy does pull through, he will never be the same.

So many lives were altered by the tragedy at the fair. It would be a difficult situation to overcome. Many of the kids would need counseling to cope with the loss of their friend. Death is hard enough to deal with as an adult, but is exceptionally hard for someone so young. Haralson County High would mourn the loss of Tabitha for quite some time to come, not to mention Randy's critical condition. He might not make it either. This is terrible.

The paramedics continued to work on Randy until he was stable enough to transport to the hospital. They called for an air flight unit to take him to a hospital in Atlanta which was better equipped to deal with the seriousness of his condition. The paramedics didn't anticipate his survival.

While Tara was standing, watching and waiting for the paramedics to release some information on Randy's condition, someone tapped her on her shoulder. She turned around and saw it was Randy's mom, Jessica Barker. She was shaking uncontrollably and she had tears running down her face. She was frantic.

"How is he? Is he okay? Is he still alive?" Jessica asked.

"Let me take you to the paramedics and you can talk to them and ask him how Randy is. They can help you. I will tell them who you are," Tara responded.

Tara took Jessica by the hand and led her to where the paramedics were taking care of her son. She explained that Jessica was Randy's mom. They were more than glad to provide Jessica with information on her son's condition. They told her they were sending him by helicopter to Grady Hospital in Atlanta, where a specialist was available to handle his case. All they could tell her at this particular time was that her son was stable, and they wouldn't know anymore until he reached the hospital

Jessica and Blake, Randy's dad, went to their car and left for the hospital. They wanted to get there as soon as they possibly could so they could speak with the doctors. This would be the longest trip the two parents had ever taken in their life. They had no idea if Randy would even survive the trip to the hospital.

"Tabitha was riding with Randy, and she died on impact. There was nothing they could do for her. I need to call Bill and Jane and see how they are, and let them know how sorry we are for their loss. Randy will be very upset at this news when he learns it. But right now we just have to pray we won't lose him too," Jessica said sobbingly.

"I feel so sorry for them. I will miss Tabitha very much. It won't be the same without her being around all of the time. She and Randy have been together for so long. Our lives will never be the same. How are we all going to deal with this tragedy? Will things ever be normal again?" Blake asked his wife.

Jessica called Bill Sealy. She needed to talk to him and let him know how things were going with Randy. She didn't know how to begin, but she wanted him to know they were there for him and Jane and they were praying for them. She couldn't imagine the shock Bill and Jane must be feeling right now. She only knew the pain of her own situation, but at least Randy was still alive for now.

"Is this Bill?" Jessica inquired.

"Yes, who is this?"

"It's me, Jessica Barker. How are you and Jane doing?"

"Jane will be in the hospital overnight. She collapsed at the scene and they want to be sure everything is okay with her. They believe the shock of the accident is probably responsible for her condition but they want to be sure. Tabitha is gone. She died on impact. I have to identify her body when they get it to the hospital. My little girl is dead!"

"I am so sorry Bill. If there is anything we can do, please let us know. We are on our way to Atlanta to be with Randy. They won't know how bad he is until they do the necessary testing. We don't know if he is going to make it or not. We are praying for you guys. We will let you know when we find out something more definite. We love you guys. We are going to miss, Tabitha so much; she was like our own child and we loved her too! It's going to be very hard to get through this but maybe we can all help each other," Jessica said.

"We love you guys too. Please, do let us know as soon as you find out how Randy is doing. We will be praying for you too! Be safe on your trip and please let Randy know we love him," Bill told her.

Jessica ended the phone call and put her face into her hands crying uncontrollably. She was so torn. The Sealy's just lost their daughter and she just kept praying for the recovery of her son. Was that acceptable? She found herself thinking she was glad Randy wasn't the one killed in the accident. As bad as it hurt for the loss of Tabitha, she knew her pain would be much more if it was her child instead.

16

❧

"Mom, we are going to Grady Hospital in Atlanta. Randy has been taken there by helicopter. He and Tabitha were riding the new roller coaster at the fair and their car flew off of the track. Tabitha was killed instantly, and they don't know if Randy is going to make it yet or not. Would you please call Kinsley and let her know what happened? Tell her Megan is going with us," Tara explained to Angela.

"Oh my God, where are their parents?" Angela asked.

"The Sealy's are at Polk Medical Center; Jane collapsed at the scene. The Barker's are on their way to the hospital to be with Randy," Tara replied.

"Okay, I'll let Kinsley know. I'll go to the hospital and offer some support to Jane and Bill. Let me know something. You guys be careful, please. I love you," Angela told her.

The six kids got into the car and started the drive to the hospital. They couldn't believe the horrendous outcome of what was supposed to be a joyous night. They lost one of their best friends and one was fighting for his life at this very moment. They were very hopeful that Randy would be able to come through this; although, judging from what they saw earlier, they weren't so sure.

There was nothing but silence and sadness between the teens on their hour and half ride to Atlanta. They were almost numb with grief. They couldn't help but think about the fact that it could have been either of them in Randy's and Tabitha's position. The mere thought scared them to death.

17

They also knew it would take them a long time to overcome this tragedy.

Jessica and Blake arrived to the hospital and immediately went to the emergency room to learn about Randy's condition. They told the nurse their son was being flown in by helicopter, from Cedartown, Georgia. The nurse asked them to take a seat while she checked the computer for Randy's location.

When the nurse pulled the chart, she quickly realized Randy needed emergency surgery to repair his spleen, some broken limbs, and to address the swelling in his brain. The nurse was given orders to notify the doctor as soon as the Barker's arrived.

"Are you the Barker's?" Dr. Hardy asked.

"Yes, we are. How is our son? How is Randy?" Jessica questioned.

"I have to be very honest with you; it doesn't look too good right now. I can't make you any promises, but your son is in desperate need of a surgery. I can tell you that without the surgery, it is very likely he will not make it. He has a ruptured spleen, two broken legs, three broken ribs, a broken arm, and a badly fractured skull. The fracture in his skull is causing pressure on his brain. We need to go in and release the swelling in order to give him a chance of survival. Once we take down the swelling we will keep him sedated giving his body a chance to recover. I need your permission before I can proceed. Time is a very important factor in your son's case," Dr. Hardy explained.

"Can we see him before you take him to surgery, please? We haven't seen him since this began," Jessica pleaded with the doctor.

"You can see him, but only for a few minutes. We need to prepare him for surgery. Follow me and I will take you to him."

When the Barker's reached the room where their son was, they were in total dismay at what they saw. He was almost unrecognizable. He was bloody from head to toe; his limbs were gruesomely distorted and he had severe cuts and bruising everywhere. The mere sight of Randy lowered his parent's hopes of his survival.

Jessica and Blake went to their son's bedside. They took his hand and told him how much they loved him. Jessica laid her head on his chest and just absorbed the sound of his breathing for fear this may be the last time she would have that privilege. *Why did this have to happen to him?* was the thought continuing to race through her mind. She couldn't go on without him. He was her baby. How would she give him up if she was forced to?

"Randy, we are here son. We love you very much. Please try to hang on and get better. We can't live without you. We need you son," Jessica sadly pleaded.

The nurse came in to take Randy to surgery. She told the Barker's they would have to return to the waiting room. She assured them she would let them know something as soon as she could.

Jessica and Blake kissed Randy on the forehead. It felt to them as if they were seeing him alive for the last time. Jessica grabbed her husband and became hysterical at the thought of their son not coming out of surgery alive. She was frantic with worry.

The other kids had arrived at the hospital by the time Jessica and Blake returned to the waiting room. They quickly rushed over to them to find out how Randy was doing. They were all very worried about their friend.

"They had to take him into surgery. We don't know if he is going to be okay yet. All we can do for him right now is pray. Thank you all so very much for coming," Jessica explained.

The kids began hugging each other for comfort and support. They all had tears running down their faces. They were hoping so hard for Randy's recovery, and now they were being told there may not be a recovery. This night was becoming more and more terrible by the second. The next few hours were going to be extremely long for everyone. The uncertainty of these circumstances was enormously hard to accept.

Chapter Three

*M*eanwhile, back in Cedartown, the crews was still working at the fair trying to clean up the scene of destruction the roller coaster left behind. The car was still lying on the ground and because of its enormous weight; the workers had to call one of the local companies in to bring some equipment sturdy enough to lift it up off of the ground.

They had already shut the fair down for the night and it was very unlikely to reopen anytime soon considering what took place. The fair owner was totally grief stricken at what was usually a fun evening of entertainment for everyone. He had to find out what caused the ride to malfunction. The ride was inspected prior to opening, and some of the workers had even ridden it. He just couldn't understand what went so wrong. He thought this would most likely be his last fair.

"Judy, where are you? Judy! Judy!" a woman's voice was calling loudly.

The woman seemed as though she was almost in a panic. The fair owner approached the young woman and he could see she had been crying. She was shaking all over.

"Ma'am, may I help you? My name is Henry, I own this fair. Everyone was ordered to leave, why are you still here?" he asked.

"I'm Rosy, I can't find my daughter. I've been looking for her for quite a while. She's five and has blonde hair and blue eyes. She's approximately three and a half feet tall and weighs about forty pounds. She was wearing a pair of jeans and a blue jacket. Will you help me find her sir?" Rosy desperately asked.

"Yes ma'am, I will be glad to help you search for your daughter. Let me notify the authorities that she is missing! They can alert everyone to be on the lookout for her. What is the little girl's name?"

"Her name is Judy. I've got to find her. I'm scared. Where could she be? I should have already found her by now. I've already called her father; he's on his way."

Henry left to alert the authorities of the little girl's disappearance and provided them with the description given by her mother. They quickly began to stop all the vehicles leaving the fairgrounds looking for the little five-year-old girl. They feared that with the distraction of the roller coaster accident, someone might have taken advantage of the emergency situation to kidnap a child.

A red convertible approached the front entrance gate attempting to enter the fairgrounds. The driver was prevented entry until he explained his wife had called him and informed him of his little girl's disappearance. The police officer immediately directed him in and told him where to find his wife.

When Rosy spotted her husband, she hurriedly ran to meet him. She was beside herself with fear. She didn't know where Judy was and they hadn't been able to find her. She had all kind of thoughts racing through her mind and none of them were good. Judy had to be safe. Maybe she was just playing hide and go seek.

"Thank God you're here. I still haven't found Judy. I don't know where she could be. I've looked everywhere. Henry, the fairs owner and the police have been assisting me in searching for her. We have to find her Daniel! We just have to!" Rosy exclaimed.

"When did you see her last, Rosy?" Daniel asked.

"I haven't seen her since all of the commotion began with the roller coaster. One teen-ager was killed and one badly injured when the car they were riding in jumped off of the track. Judy was there just prior to that, but then I couldn't find her shortly after. I'm scared, Daniel."

"So it's been a while since you actually saw her, right?"

"Yes, and I can't imagine where she could be. I have absolutely checked everywhere. I don't know anywhere on these grounds I haven't already checked."

"Just try to stay calm. We'll find her. She has to be here somewhere. You go that way and I'll go this way. We'll meet back here in fifteen minutes," Daniel told his wife.

Rosy and Daniel began to search for their daughter. They were terrified they couldn't find their daughter and they hoped she was unharmed. They couldn't help but think someone might have taken her from the fairgrounds. They were hopeful she would turn up soon.

The loud sound of the crane made it hard to hear anything. The crew was using the crane to lift the car that jumped the track with the two teens aboard. Everyone who wasn't helping lift the car was looking for little Judy Thornton. They hoped the loud sound of the equipment wouldn't prevent them being able to hear her if she answered them.

All of a sudden the loud roar of the motor came to an abrupt halt as the crane operator made a gruesome discovery when the car cleared the pavement.

There was a small body underneath the wreckage. When they approached they realized it matched the description of the child everyone was searching for. The clothes, hair color, height and weight all matched the description of Judy Thornton.

"Sir, I need you over here pronto. I have an emergency situation at the accident site. You're not going to believe this," Raleigh told his boss.

"Be right there. Why did you stop the crane? Are you through clearing the car away?" Henry asked.

"You'll see sir. I don't want to tell you on the radio, you have to come and see this."

When Henry reached the crane, he couldn't understand why the men were just standing around, when the car was still hanging in the air. It was their job to clear it completely away. When he got close enough to see what was going on, he understood why the work came to a standstill. He could see the little body, badly mangled on the ground.

Apparently, when the car left the track flying through the air, the little girl was standing where it landed. She was so small that she was completely concealed beneath the car. No one ever noticed the child was standing exactly where the car landed. It was undeniably Judy Thornton based on the description her mother provided. How were they going to explain this?

Officer Johnson was the investigating officer; he was left with the heart wrenching chore of informing the child's parents of the discovery. This was by a long shot the hardest part of the job. He had no doubt the Thornton's were going to fall apart when they learned of their daughter's death. Nevertheless, he knew he still had to tell them.

"Mr. and Mrs. Thornton, my name is Officer Mack Johnson. I am the officer in charge here. I have some bad news for you. I'm terribly sorry, but we found Judy. She was standing where the roller coaster car landed. When we lifted the car up we found her body underneath. She is dead. We will need you to identify her."

"No, No, No, not my baby! She has to be alive! I know she's okay, you're lying to us! Why are you lying to us?" Rosy shouted hysterically.

Daniel just stood there in silence. He didn't even know how he should react. He was in complete disbelief. Could Judy really be dead? He couldn't believe what the officer just said.

"Take me to her, officer. I will identify her. Please, tell me that you could be mistaken. My baby can't be dead," Daniel said.

As Daniel walked up to his daughter's body, he knew right away the nightmare was reality. His little girl's body lay crumbled on the ground in somewhat of a trench, where the heavy steel car landed on top of her. She was lifeless with her blonde hair soaked red with blood, and her limbs twisted in grotesque positions. How did this happen? Who was responsible for the death of his child? Someone had to pay for this and he wanted to know who it would be.

Daniel picked his little girl up and he held her in his arms. He stroked her hair and told her everything was going to be alright. He kept telling her over and over again, how much he loved her. He cried so heavily, his tears washed away some of the blood on his daughter's face.

"Would someone please explain to me how this could happen? My baby has been here buried beneath this pile of steel, and no one even knew she was here! Tell me how! Oh God, Judy is dead! Oh God, please help me!" Daniel began to frantically scream.

No one could offer him an explanation. They were confounded themselves. The tragedy at the fair claimed two lives already and it may well be three by the time it's over. This was a horrible catastrophe that unquestionably altered many lives. The question now was, how did this happen?

Dave Jackson was on duty tonight and he was helping at the fair. He was absolutely taken aback by what happened. Was this a terrible freak accident or something else? Surely no one caused this on purpose, did they? He decided to call Angela and let her know what was going on.

"You are not going to believe how this thing at the fair has ended up," Dave told his wife.

"What do you mean? What happened?"

"When we lifted up the roller coaster car we found a little girl underneath it. It was the Thornton's daughter Judy, the little five-year-old. This night just gets worse and worse."

"Oh no! How did that happen? Did they just now find her?"

"Yeah, we just found her a few minutes ago. This is the most terrible thing I have ever dealt with in my entire career. This is crazy."

"I haven't heard anything from the kids about Randy. I don't know how he is doing. I went to the hospital to see the Sealy's and they're taking Tabitha's death really hard. I feel horrible for all of them. Let me know if anything changes. Do you know what caused the roller coaster to malfunction yet?" Angela asked.

"No not yet, we're roping off the scene and then we will begin to investigate the cause. I'll let you know, I gotta go. I love you. Let me know something when you hear about Randy's condition. I hope he will recover."

This small town was definitely raging with grief. The news would travel quickly. Everyone was in a state of panic. What in the world was the reason for something so unspeakable? This, or nothing like it, had ever happened in Cedartown before.

✑ Chapter Four ✑

The Barkers were anxiously awaiting news of Randy's condition. No one had updated them on his condition for hours. The only thing they felt sure of is he must still be hanging on, since no one came to inform them of his passing. They knew it was going to be a long while before the doctor finished with their son especially considering the extent of his injuries.

Tara, Megan, Grace, Tank, Jake, and James were sacked out everywhere awaiting word from the doctor. They didn't want to leave until they made sure their friend would be okay. They didn't have to attend school tomorrow, so they could afford a loss of sleep.

Suddenly a loudspeaker sounded, startling them awake. The horror of its sound was even more bloodcurdling when it announced there was a code blue somewhere in the hospital. The first thought that crossed everyone's mind was that it might be Randy. Jessica began to cry praying the alert was not for her son.

Blake decided to go to the nurse's station and see if he could get an update on their son's condition. It had been four grueling hours and they hadn't heard anything. Someone must know something.

"Excuse me, my name is Blake Barker, my son went into surgery hours ago. We haven't heard anything about him. Dr. Hardy is his doctor. Would you please check and let us know something?"

"I will see what I can find out sir and I will let you know," the nurse responded

"Thank you very much, I appreciate it ma'am."

Blake sat down with his wife. He knew he needed to stay close to her and comfort her as much as he could. He was falling apart on the inside but he had to remain calm and collected on the outside. He would wait until all of this was over and then he would do his panicking. He and Jessica were becoming very restless wondering how Randy was doing.

"Do you guys want to go and get something to drink?" Megan asked her friends.

They were overwhelmed with worry too. They didn't want to upset Randy's parents, so they tried their best to hold themselves together. They needed to take a walk to burn up some of their helplessness. They didn't want Randy to die too. They already had to face life without Tabitha, and they didn't want to be forced to continue on without Randy as well.

"Hello?" Tara answered.

"Have you guys heard anything yet?" Angela asked her daughter.

"No, not yet, but hopefully we will soon."

"Your father was working the scene at the fair tonight. After everyone left; they were cleaning up. You'll never guess what they discovered."

"What?"

"When they raised the roller coaster car they found the Thornton's daughter. She was pinned beneath it. They didn't even know she was there until they lifted up the car."

"Are you serious? I know little Judy, she is the little blonde haired girl. She's very sweet. How did that happen?" Tara asked.

"She was standing where the car landed on the pavement. Everyone was so pre-occupied they didn't notice she was there. She was so small she couldn't be seen with the car on top of her. Her mother was searching for her, but she thought maybe she was just hiding from her. They are in bad shape of course. This whole thing is awful. Let me know as soon as you hear something dear. I need to go, I love you," Angela said.

"I love you too, Mom. Thank you for telling me about Judy. If you happen to talk to the Thornton's will you please tell them I am so sorry for their loss?"

☙

"You guys are never going to believe this!" Tara told them.

"What is it, Tara?" Megan questioned.

"When the car flew off of the coaster track it landed on a five-year-old little girl."

"Who was it?" Grace asked.

"It was the Thornton's daughter. She's dead. The weight of the car crushed her. They just found her not long ago. Her parents were searching for her thinking she was just hiding from them. But she was beneath the steel car instead," Tara told them.

30

"This is unreal! How did this happen. This night started out as fun but it sure didn't end that way," James stated.

The teens headed back to the waiting room where they continued to sit with Randy's parents waiting to hear something about his condition. They immediately noticed that Blake was embracing his wife tightly in an effort to calm her. She was considerably upset. They guessed that the doctor may have come in with some bad news while they were gone.

"Is Randy okay Mrs. Barker?" Tank asked.

"The doctor came out and talked with us while you were gone. He said Randy would probably never walk again due to a spinal injury he sustained. He also said the next twenty-four hours were very crucial. It can go either way right now. He's not out of the woods yet. They said he might have some permanent brain damage as well," Jessica explained to the kids.

Hearing the news, all the kids broke down. They had held it in as long as they could. They loved Randy and this was awful news. His entire life had turned upside down in a matter of a few short moments. None of them could fathom such a gut wrenching result. They felt badly for Randy and his parents. Their lives would definitely be altered in a huge way from this point on.

All the teens felt so helpless. There was nothing they could do to help. They wanted to take away this terrible tragedy and turn it in to something wonderful. Unfortunately, there was no way for them to do that. This was breaking their hearts in two. They knew they narrowly escaped the same circumstances, or worse, themselves. They felt lucky to be alive and well, but felt guilty at the same time.

The doctors informed Jessica and Blake they were taking Randy to the intensive care unit, so they could keep an exceptionally close eye on him. No one but his parents would be allowed to go in to see him due to his critical condition. The kids hugged Jessica and Blake and told them to tell Randy they loved him. They decided to go home since they couldn't be any help there at the hospital.

Jane Sealy regained consciousness for the first time since her collapse at the scene of the accident. She quickly remembered what brought her to the hospital to begin with and she began to cry uncontrollably. She became so hysterical the nurse administered another sedative to calm her nerves. She wasn't dealing well with Tabitha's death.

"Mr. Sealy, there is an officer at the nurse's station. He asked me to come get you. Your daughter's body just arrived to the hospital. I understand they need you to identify her," the nurse inquired.

Bill asked her to lead him to the officer. She took him to the nurse's station where the officer was waiting for him. He was holding his hat in his hand. It was Officer Dave Jackson.

"I am so sorry, Bill. If there is anything I can do and I mean anything at all, please let me know. How is Jane?" Dave asked his friend.

"She woke up but they had to put her back under. She is still in shock. I am worried about her at this point. She and Tabitha were so close. They did everything together. This is going to be so hard for her. I don't know if she will ever be able to get over it."

"I can't imagine the overwhelming pain you two must be feeling right now. I am so, so, sorry," Dave said.

"Do they know what caused the accident yet, Dave?"

"No not yet, but we made another gruesome discovery while we were cleaning the debris up."

"What did you find?"

"When we raised the car, we found little Judy Thornton underneath it. She was dead. She had been there the whole time. No one saw her when the car fell on her, and you couldn't see her being beneath it because she was too small," Dave told him.

"That's terrible. That poor little girl; those poor parents, I feel horrible for them. I can't believe any of this! Have you heard anything about Randy Barker yet?"

"Nothing yet, but Angela is supposed to let me know as soon as she finds out anything. I will let you know," Dave assured him.

"Thanks a lot Dave. I really appreciate that. I guess you better take me to see Tabitha now," Bill insisted. He wanted to get this over with. He had no doubt that this would be his hardest task yet.

When he entered the room his stomach started to turn flips. He literally felt sick at the thought of what he was about to do, but he had no choice. When Dave pulled back the sheet, Bill quickly informed him that this was indeed his daughter. He asked Dave if he could have some time alone with his little girl. Dave told him to take as long as he needed and he would wait outside the door.

Bill stood over his daughter with the reality of this being his last private moment with her. He loved Tabitha so much and this was tearing his insides out. How was he to carry on with the absence of his baby girl? He wasn't so sure he was going to be able to leave her here alone. He couldn't stand the thought of turning his back on her and walking away without her following him.

"Oh baby, I am going to miss you so much. You are my beautiful little girl and I don't want to go on without you. I just can't imagine my life without your presence. You will always be with me in my heart and mind. I will never, ever, forget you. You mean so much to me. Did I tell you how much I love you baby? I know you're in heaven because you were such an angel. I wish you didn't have to go; can't you just stay with Daddy and Mommy? We need you so much. Please don't leave us!" Bill pleaded with his daughter's lifeless body.

Bill held up as long as his heart would allow him, and then lost all control of his emotions. He couldn't believe his daughter was gone forever. A daughter that he had loved so much; he was so proud of her. How could this happen? Bill just couldn't find a reason good enough to ease his pain and suffering for Tabitha's death.

The lives of three families were turned completely upside down by a single event at the county fair. This was so crazy. Life seemed very unfair to the Barker's, the Sealy's, and the Thornton's, right now. How would they ever be able to understand this freak accident? It had claimed the most important treasure of their lives.

Chapter Five

*T*he tragic news of the fair accident made the front page of The Cedartown Standard on Saturday morning. It also made the front page of The Gateway Beacon in Buchanan and the Rome News Tribune as well. Not to mention all the local television stations.

The stories gave a full account of the terrible failure of the new roller coaster ride at the Polk County fair. It explained the loss of the two young lives and one still hanging in the balance, and the fact that the authorities were investigating to find out the cause. Henry Fuller, the fairs owner was also conducting an investigation into the cause of the accident.

Henry was extremely disturbed by the prior night's events. He had owned the fair for thirty years and not once had anything like this ever taken place. He was completely horrified at what happened. He had to be sure this was not negligence in any way on his part. He couldn't stand the thought that he may have done something to cause it.

The obituary column was a sad reminder of the precious lives claimed by the strange episode that unfolded the night before.

Ms. Tabitha Elaine Sealy, age eighteen, of 311 Lee Rd., Felton, Georgia, and Judy Madison Thornton, age five, of 212 Rainey Lake Rd., Felton, Georgia were killed in a roller coaster accident at the county fair. Their services will be held on Monday.

The school gave a day off with excuse to anyone who wanted to attend the funerals.

All the stores were taking donations for the families to ease their expenses. Hopefully, they would be able to raise enough money to more than pay for the costs. Everyone wanted to help however they could, but other than collecting money they were unclear as to what they might be able to do without overstepping their boundaries.

Jane was still in the hospital, and hadn't yet been able to come to terms with the loss of her daughter. She built her whole life around her and now with Tabitha's passing, she felt she had no purpose or will to live. Bill was extremely worried for her well-being and felt completely helpless.

Bill lost his eighteen-year-old daughter last night, and now it felt as though he was also losing his wife. This entire thing was a disaster. He didn't even know how he would be able to get on with life with the loss of his daughter, and how was he supposed to make it without his wife? He was really starting to lose it.

"Bill, where is Tabitha?" Jane asked.

"You remember Jane; she was in a terrible accident at the fair. She's gone."

"I know, but where is she? Where did they take her?"

"They took her to Lester C. Litesey's funeral home. They are preparing her for the funeral."

"What are we going to do Bill? How are we supposed to go on without Tabitha? She was my life. She was my baby! I don't want to live without her! I should have gone

36

first. Children aren't supposed to die before their parents; it's just not meant to be that way! Why did this have to happen to us?" Jane asked sobbingly.

Bill had no idea how to respond, especially when he was feeling much the same way. He didn't understand either. He thought that he and Jane would go first. Tabitha would attend their funerals, but not this way. They would never have any grandchildren to adore and love. Their daughter's life ended quicker than it began, and most certainly more unexpectedly.

"I don't know what we are going to do Jane, but we have to think about what Tabitha would want us to do. She would want us to find a way to go on. You know how she was. She knew how much we loved her and she knows we are going to miss her tremendously, but she wouldn't want us to just give up. I know she wouldn't."

"I know you're right Bill, I just don't know how to do that. It's going to take me a long time to get over this. I don't think I ever will. I want to wake up from this nightmare and hear my little girl telling me everything is going to be okay."

Bill embraced her to console her. He could feel her pain merging with his own. The heartbreak he felt was deep. There was no way to explain the mixed emotions they were experiencing. They were hurting immeasurably but were very angry also. They needed some explanation to help them understand this horrible circumstance.

"The doctor said he would let you go home tomorrow, if you did okay today Jane. You have to concentrate on your own health right now. We have to get you out of here so you can attend Tabitha's memorial service. She would definitely want you to be there," Bill encouraged his wife.

In the meantime, the Thornton's were trying to deal with their loss as well. Their little girl had barely lived and now her life was over, and they could only wonder why. Rosy was expecting another child in a few months. She and Daniel looked forward to the arrival of their second child, unaware that it would be their only child.

Daniel was clinging close to his wife in this crisis. He was afraid that the stress might cause some complications with her pregnancy. He couldn't bear the thought of losing another child before it even arrived. The doctors hadn't told them what the baby was going to be yet, but they were hoping for another little girl. They knew this baby would never take the place of the child they just lost, but hopefully would relieve some of the pain they were feeling.

Daniel could hear Rosy crying and sobbing. She was lying across the bed with a picture of Judy. She was holding the picture close and was calling her daughter's name over and over. Occasionally, she would pull the picture away from her chest so she could look at it. This brought even more pain and sorrow. Little Judy was gone and there was no way to bring her back. Why did she die? This wasn't fair at all. She would never be able to graduate, get married, have children, or any of the things people experience in their lifetime.

Daniel went to his wife, pulled her close to him and cried with her. He was more heartbroken than he could ever remember. His dad died a couple of years earlier and recalling the pain he had suffered, it didn't compare to what he was feeling now. How would he ever get over this? He saw no light at the end of the tunnel. This cloud did not have a silver lining, and if it did he couldn't see it.

There was a knock on the door, and when Daniel opened it, his mother-in-law was standing there and had obviously been crying as her eyes were red and swollen. He invited her in as she grabbed him and hugged him close to her. The tears began to flow.

"I am so sorry. I can't believe this happened to our little Judy. How could something so horrible happen to such a sweet baby girl?" Carmen asked.

Carmen had always been close with her daughter. When Judy was born, it was one of the most exciting nights she could ever remember. She was the sweetest most precious little girl she had ever laid her eyes on. From that very moment she loved her with everything inside her. She couldn't accept that she was gone now without any warning.

"Where is Rosy? Is she alright? I know she is taking this whole thing very hard. She loved that little girl so very much. You both did. I'm so sorry. I wish there was something I could say or do to help, but I know there isn't. If you do think of something please let me know, Daniel." Carmen made her son-in-law promise.

Daniel led Carmen into the bedroom where Rosy was. She was still lying on the bed holding her daughter's picture to her chest. Carmen walked over and embraced her tightly as Rosy cried on her mother's shoulder. Carmen wished there was some way she could take away some of her daughter's pain, but unfortunately there wasn't.

"Oh mama, my baby is dead! My little girl is gone! What am I going to do mama? Please help me ease this pain! It hurts so badly! I want my baby back! Why did this have to happen to her?" Rosy sadly pleaded.

"I'm so, so sorry dear. I know how much you loved her. I can't even imagine what you must be going through right now. I am here for you, and will always be here for you no matter what. I will do whatever I can to help you; just let me know what I can do," Carmen reassured her.

Daniel had to leave the room as he couldn't bear to see the wife he loved in such grief. He was overwhelmed by his own anguish and sorrow. He couldn't get the image out of his mind of his daughter's bloody broken body lying on the ground.

Daniel was trying exceptionally hard not to blame his wife for Judy's death. He couldn't help but wonder how she could lose track of her whereabouts at the fair. If she had only been holding her hand, she wouldn't have been standing there alone when the car came off of the track. Why didn't she keep her with her? How could she leave their little girl alone?

Daniel knew his wife did not intentionally allow their baby to be killed. He knew how much she loved her and he could plainly see the pain she was feeling now. What if she was thinking the same thing? He hoped she wasn't. He would never speak these thoughts out loud, especially not in the presence of his wife.

There was another knock on the door and this time it was Jenny Thornton, Daniel's mom. He opened the door and she took hold of him and hugged him very securely next to her. She burst into tears and began crying loudly. She was trembling all over. They stood there crying together on each other's shoulders.

"How are you Daniel? Are you alright? Is there anything I can do for you? I love you son. I am so sorry! I loved that little girl so much!" Jenny told him.

"Can you give me back my little girl? That's the only thing I want. I want this whole nightmare to come to an end! This can't be real!" Daniel shouted.

Jenny held her son even closer to ease some of the anguish he was feeling. If only she could roll back the hands of time she would gladly do it, but that wasn't possible. They say there is a reason for everything that happens, but what reason could there be for this awful thing? What had they done to deserve this? This was the question the family continued to ask themselves, and nothing seemed to be an appropriate answer.

In two days they would be putting Judy's body in the ground, and every trace of her physical being would be gone. Pictures would be their only comfort after that; pictures and their own personal memories of their precious child. It seemed like just yesterday when she was born and now her life was over. Nothing would ever be the same again for the Thornton's.

Henry Fuller was extremely distraught over the accident. He knew there was no way to bring the children back, but there had to be something he could do to help the families. He decided he would pay the cost of the two girl's final expenses, and would contribute to Randy's hospital bill.

Henry didn't want the families to have the worry of a financial burden during this ordeal.

Henry gathered the information from the papers about the location of where the girl's would be put to rest and which funeral home would be handling the arrangements. He knew the owner of the business very well, so he placed a personal phone call making arrangements to pay all the costs. He also called the hospital in Atlanta where Randy was, making the same arrangement.

There still wasn't any word from the police about the investigation results. The mystery of the cause of the accident was still not solved.

While Henry was walking the fairgrounds searching for anything that would help determine the cause of the accident, he spotted something very peculiar. Lying on the ground in the bushes next to the ride he found the pin that used to hold the cars together. What did this mean?

Henry hadn't given much thought to the people he saw at the scene the night before, until just now. He completely forgot about seeing Kirk Cannon, who was a former employee Henry fired two days earlier. Could he possibly have something to do with this horrible accident?

"Can I speak to Officer Johnson, please? It's very important," Henry asked.

"One moment please."

"This is Officer Johnson, may I help you?"

"This is Henry Fuller. As I was walking around the fairgrounds I found something I believe may be very important. I also remembered something else that could be very helpful. I need to see you as soon as possible. I'll wait for you here at the fairgrounds," Henry told him.

"I'll be right there, Henry."

Chapter Six

*R*andy Barker was still in the intensive care unit at Grady Hospital and there was no change in his condition. He was still extremely critical. His parents remained at his side patiently waiting for him to regain consciousness. They continued to pray for his recovery.

The intensive care unit only permitted visitation every four hours, so Jessica and Blake Barker made themselves at home in the waiting room and hadn't been home at all. They were afraid to leave their son's side fearing something might happen where they would be needed.

The family gathered to comfort them in their time of need. They were trying to keep Blake and Jessica preoccupied as much as possible in the hope of easing their discomfort and pain. The Barker's had always been a very close knit family.

"Do you want me to get you something to eat?" Jerry Barker asked his brother and sister-in-law.

"I'm not hungry, but thank you very much Jerry," Jessica replied.

"I'm not either," Blake responded.

"The two of you haven't eaten anything since you've been here, so I am going to get you something to eat anyway. Maybe you will feel like eating it later. You need to keep your strength up for Randy. The last thing we need is for you to get sick!" Jerry expressed.

Jessica and Blake knew Jerry was right. They really did need to eat something, but they just couldn't. Their nerves were too upset to even consider it. It wasn't long until visiting hours and they would be able to go in and see Randy.

Jessica spotted Dr. Hardy as he came out of the ICU doors headed in their direction. She wondered if he had some new information. She hoped it would be news of an improvement in Randy's condition.

"Mr. and Mrs. Barker, I am still taking care of your son. I will be his doctor for the duration of his stay with us. He hasn't regained consciousness yet as we still have him sedated allowing the swelling around his brain to go down. With head injuries of this nature, patients sometimes tend to become combative when they awake causing more trauma. That's why we want him to stay asleep until the swelling goes down," The doctor explained.

"Is there any change at all, Doctor?" Blake questioned.

"We had a situation a short while ago when he went into cardiac arrest, but fortunately we were able to restart his heart without a problem. He is stable for now and hopefully that will continue to be the case. We are monitoring him very closely. We will let you know if anything changes. You can go back and see him now if you wish," Dr. Hardy told the parents.

"What is his chance of recovery doctor? Is he going to be okay or not?" Jessica asked.

"I can't answer that at this point; I don't know for sure. We are doing all we can," The doctor assured them.

Jessica reached around her husband's neck and she began to squeeze him as tightly as she could. She was horrified at the news of her son's cardiac arrest. Was he going to make it through this? If he did, how severe would the consequences be? Things just kept getting more and more dim.

Blake helped his wife to Randy's room. They wanted to stay with him as long as the nurse would allow. They didn't know from one minute to the next if he would still be with them or not. He was fighting hard, but did he have the strength he needed to rise above the trauma? That was the immediate question.

"Randy, it's Mom and Dad. How are you feeling? The whole family is in the waiting room and they said to tell you they love you very much. Your friends were here last night and they said to tell you they love you, too," Jessica told her son.

Randy looked so pitiful. He had tubes going in every direction and was purple all over from the cuts and bruises. He had stitches in various places, and both his legs were in traction in addition to a cast on his arm. He had bandages wrapped around his head from the surgery to relieve the pressure around his brain. He didn't even look like Randy.

Jessica stood at her son's bedside with his hand held tightly in hers, holding on for dear life. She didn't want to let go for fear that she would never be able to hold his hand again.

Suddenly, Randy let out the shrillest gut wrenching sound.

"Tabitha! Tabitha! Where is she? Where is my girlfriend?" Randy screamed.

The nurse rushed in immediately with a syringe in her hand. It was filled with a sedative to calm his agitation. He was extremely belligerent, and even though he was restrained to the bed the nurse still had to call for help trying to give him the shot. He was flailing all over the bed risking further injury and trauma.

Another nurse bolted through the door and immediately realized what was happening. She quickly assisted in giving Randy the shot to calm him down. The Barker's stood back in shock as they watched their son's unusual behavior. They couldn't believe it.

The nurses finally managed to give Randy the shot, and he instantly became calm again. Afraid of another outburst, the nurse asked his parents to return to the waiting room. The nurse didn't want the parents to witness another episode, knowing it was difficult for them to see. She told them she was sorry, and promised to inform them of any further change in their son's condition.

Jessica was more distraught now than she was when she first entered her son's room. She had never seen anything like this before, and was now even more so worried that he may never fully recover.

What did life have in store for Randy? He was so alive and full of energy before all of this took place. Would he ever again be himself? Would he be able to graduate? What quality of life would Randy have if he managed to survive?

When Jessica and Blake went back to the waiting room, they explained to their families what happened. They were all concerned with the heavy burden Jessica and Blake were carrying. The realization that Randy may never come out of this was plain to see, and even if he did make it his life would likely be seriously altered.

Randy's friends were filled with anxiety about his condition. They hadn't spoken with either of his parents today, and had no idea how he was doing. Tara decided to call Jessica and check on Randy's status. She hoped things had improved during the night.

"Mrs. Barker, this is Tara. How is Randy doing today?"

"He's not doing well at all Tara. There's been no improvement, but the doctor is hopeful he will start to show some progress soon."

"I won't keep you ma'am, I just wanted to call and check on him. We are all praying for his recovery," Tara responded.

Tara was very disappointed that Randy showed no improvement since they left the hospital last night. She was afraid he was going to die just like Tabitha had. When was this repulsion going to let up? The end seemed nowhere in sight.

Tara called Megan to update her on the news about Randy. Megan was her best friend and she needed to talk to her. What if it had been her who died? This alarming thought continually popped into Tara's head. This whole situation gave her a new appreciation for the people in her life whom she cared about. She realized they could be gone in an instant without warning.

"Hey, what were you doing?" Tara asked Megan.

"I was just sitting here with my mom. We were talking about all of the craziness that happened last night. Have you heard anything about Randy today?"

"I just talked to his mom. She says he is no better today. He is still in very serious condition. They still don't know for sure if he will make it or not," Tara explained.

Tara and Megan were planning on going to the flower shop and ordering some flowers for Tabitha and the little Thornton girl. They wanted to send them to the families. They also wanted to get some flowers for Randy and have them sent to the hospital. That's the least they felt they could do.

Kinsley Keys was on duty at the hospital when they brought in Tabitha's and Judy's bodies. She was horrified by the tragedy. She remembered how she felt on the night that Jason was shot and killed. The pain was unbearable, but she couldn't imagine the depth of agony from the loss of a child. She was overwhelmed at the unimaginable thought of something so horrible.

"Megan, take this money and put it in the flowers that you are buying for the families. Let me know if there is anything else we can do to help. See if you can find out where they are taking donations so we can make a contribution," Kinsley told her daughter.

"Okay Mom, I will. Thank you! I love you."

❧

The investigation was taking a swift turn. It revealed carelessness on someone's part; although apparently not from the fair's owner or any of the current employees.

"Officer Johnson, I've been waiting for you. I have some interesting information concerning the case," Henry said.

"Oh yeah, what did you find?"

"I was walking around the Jumble Jack roller coaster, and over there close to the bushes I found this," Henry explained, holding up a large bolt.

"What is it?"

"It's the bolt that attached the runaway car to the rest of the cars on the ride. I also remember seeing Kirk Cannon in this exact area last night."

"Who is he?"

"He was one of my employees. I ordered everyone to take a drug test the day before the fair opening and Kirk failed it. He tested positive for meth, so I had to let him go. He told me he would get me before it was over, but I didn't pay much attention to him. I just figured he was upset with being fired. He was told to stay off of the fairgrounds, but I saw him here last night."

"Where does this Kirk live?" the officer asked.

"He lives with his mom at 356 College St., here in Cedartown. I hope I am wrong about this. I would hate to find out this horrible incident was caused on purpose just because some kid got angry that I fired him."

"Thanks for the information Henry, I'll check it out."

Officer Johnson drove to 356 College St. in search of Kirk Cannon. As he pulled in front of the home, he spotted someone running from the rear of the house. He immediately called for backup and proceeded to pursue the suspect on foot.

He chased him through the bushes in the yard and was now close behind him. Officer Johnson wasn't about to let him get away. He could tell by the description he had that he was in pursuit of Kirk Cannon. Why was he running if he had nothing to hide? He hadn't even had a chance to question him yet.

Knowing it was only a bluff, but hoping it would stop him, the officer yelled, "Freeze or I'll shoot! You better stop right where you are. Polk County Police, I said stop now!"

Kirk continued to run even faster and was determined to get away no doubt, but he wasn't going to if Officer Johnson had his way. He continued to run after him, when all of a sudden Kirk ran into the street and was hit by a car.

Kirk was hit by one of the police cars responding to the request for backup. When Officer Johnson approached him lying in the street, he saw that Kirk wasn't moving. He immediately checked his pulse and respiration and noted they were absent. His pupils were fixed and dilated. Kirk was dead.

The officers searched the body and the identification in his wallet confirmed it was indeed Kirk Cannon. In his pocket, they also found a piece of cable that resembled the ones used to hold the roller coaster cars together at the fair.

They marked the cable as evidence inserting it into a plastic bag and brought it to the station for further examination.

Officer Johnson decided to call Henry and give him the news of the latest developments in the case. He wanted to personally call him because he was the one who provided the information about Kirk as a potential suspect. If his assumption was right, the case at the fair had just been solved.

"Is this Henry?"

"Yes it is. Who is this?"

"It's Officer Mack Johnson. I just wanted to inform you that we found Kirk Cannon. He's dead."

"What happened to him?" Henry inquired.

"When I went to his house, he ran out the back door, and as I was chasing him he ran into the street and was hit and killed by one of our police cars. When we searched him we found a piece of cable that looks like the ones used on the roller coaster cars. We are going to examine it and see if it matches the ones on the other cars. I will let you know something when I find out for sure."

"Thank you for calling me officer, I appreciate it very much."

This information seriously turned Henry's stomach. If the piece of cable found on Kirk matched the ones used on the cars, it meant that this horrible gruesome situation was no accident at all, and the ride was intentionally sabotaged. Those poor kids lost their lives because of one person's vendetta against him. This was awful.

Chapter Seven

Today was Monday and the feeling of grief and sadness was flowing strongly in the air in the small town of Felton, Georgia. Today was the day of the children's funerals and everyone dreaded having to say good bye to their friends. They would be terribly missed by everyone.

Tabitha's service would be first and Judy's would be a few hours later. Both services were being held at the same funeral home. The entire town would be in attendance at both ceremonies. They wanted to lend as much support as they could to the grieving parents and families.

Blake would also be in attendance at the funerals. Jessica would remain at the hospital with Randy. Circumstances wouldn't allow them the convenience of being at the memorial services together. Jessica sent her condolences with her husband and told him to be sure to express them to the families for her.

It was still early and the funeral home was already extremely crowded. There were so many people that the chapel's doors were forced open to accommodate the large number of people gathered for this sad event. Felton was a small community where everyone knew everyone. They always pulled together in a time of crisis gladly lending support for their friends.

Tabitha's ceremony was to begin shortly and her mother was in shambles. She didn't know if she would be able to hold up or not. She couldn't stand the thought of walking around her daughter's casket for the last time knowing that she would never see her again. Bill had his own doubts as well. He had held up all this time, but he wasn't so sure what today held in store.

Some kids from school agreed to be pallbearers for Tabitha. This was the last thing they would be able to do for their friend, so they insisted on carrying her to her resting place. Her father was too grief stricken to be a pallbearer.

The chapel was filled with beautiful flowers. There were so many they couldn't place them all up front, and had to place some in the back. For the short while that Tabitha Elaine Sealy had lived, she made a huge impact on the lives of others. There wasn't a dry eye in the place.

The music started to play and you could hear loud sobbing all over the chapel. The goodbye lullabies were always hard to hear. It always seemed as if you were forced to sum up an entire lifetime in an hour or two. It just wasn't possible.

The Reverend approached the podium and he began the service.

"Friends, family, we are here today to mourn the passing of a lovely young girl. As you can see around you she was very much loved and will be greatly missed. This is an appointment that we all must eventually keep. It's a very sad occasion indeed. Tabitha's life was taken away by tragedy. I can't tell you why, nor do I expect you to understand. All I can tell you is that God had a purpose for this life, much the same way that he also had a purpose for its ending. I know many of you will struggle with this loss for some time to come. It's not easy to say goodbye to someone

we've all come to love and adore so much. I do hope that each one of you can find a way to go on, and learn to appreciate the time we were given to enjoy this precious life, that is no longer with us."

The music began to play again. The sobbing started again becoming even louder than before. Boxes of napkins were being handed down every aisle.

Grace Fredlander had asked Jane, before the ceremony if she could say a poem for her friend. Jane agreed to allow Grace to recite the poem in front of the crowd in remembrance of her daughter.

"Grace, would you come up here please?" the pastor asked.

Grace rose and went to the front of the chapel. She had to do this for Tabitha. She loved her very much and would never be able to do anything for her ever again. She had to do this.

"I have written a poem for Tabitha, and I wanted to share it with everyone. I loved Tabitha and I will never forget her. Her memory will live on with me forever more. I will read the poem now."

"Heaven is smiling down on our tears, our sorrow, and our pain.

They know that our heartbreak, our grief, and sadness, is now their precious gain.

You no longer live in this sinful world, where tragedy often abides.

*Just spread your wings, you beautiful girl,
and sweetly, freely fly."*

Grace finished, and returning to her seat she was crying so hard she could barely see where she was going. She would miss Tabitha greatly and she was inconsolable. It was hard for her to comprehend that her friend had met her death in such a tragic way. She died a horrible death and although she died instantly, the thought was still hard to grasp. It seemed so cruel.

The music once again started and the ushers directed the congregation to the coffin for a final view of the little girl. The congregation was overcome with sorrow and pain. They loved Tabitha and couldn't help imagining themselves in the place of the Sealy's. They felt so bad for them. There was nothing any of them could do to make it better. All they could do was surround them with love and support.

Once the congregation had taken a final walk by the casket, it was Bill's and Jane's time to bid their daughter a farewell. They could feel their knees getting weaker and weaker. How could they tell Tabitha goodbye? If they did they would never see her again. They were not prepared to walk away never seeing her again. They walked up to view their daughter, hand in hand. This was to be the longest walk they would ever take. This was it, and they couldn't believe Tabitha was really gone. This nightmare was real.

As Jane stood in front of her daughter's coffin, she bent down kissing her on the forehead. She began stroking her hair and laid her head on Tabitha's chest and began to cry uncontrollably. Bill broke down with her and together they could hardly stand on their own. They refused to move away from Tabitha. They didn't want the usher's to take her away.

"Please baby, get up! Let's go home. Mama can't make it without you! You have to get up Tabitha, you have to! Remember, we're supposed to go and pick out your prom dress soon. It's not long until graduation and then you and Randy are going to be married in August! Don't leave me Tabitha, please don't leave me!" Jane screamed in desperation.

Bill tried to pull his wife up and away from the casket, but she wasn't budging. He needed help to take her out of the chapel. He couldn't let her be there when they closed the lid to Tabitha's coffin. He wasn't ready for that himself. He had to get her to the car. He had to get out of there quickly.

Finally along with some of the other men in the chapel, Bill managed to get his wife outside. The chaplains then closed Tabitha's casket and called for the pallbearers to carry her to the hearse. This was the saddest thing some of them had ever witnessed. The desperation of Tabitha's mother was heartbreaking and miserable for everyone. They were doubtful she would be able to get over her loss.

Bill got Jane into the family car which would follow the hearse to the graveside in the long ride. There were cars literally lined up from one end of town to the other. The Sealy's were laying their daughter to rest at Sander's Cemetery and although, it wasn't that far, it seemed as though it took hours to get there. This was the loneliest ride the Sealy's had ever taken in their life.

When they arrived at the memorial park, Bill helped his wife to the chairs that the ushers had lined up in front of their daughter's grave. They were seated in the front row directly in front of the casket. Everyone began to sing Amazing Grace immediately following a few words and a heartfelt prayer from the minister.

Everyone lined past the front row to graciously offer the Sealy's their sympathy. They hugged them reminding them that they were here for them if they needed anything. There wasn't anything anyone could do for them, except be there when they needed someone.

Jane just sat there in silence and hadn't left her daughter's side. She just couldn't bring herself to leave. The cemetery employees told the Sealy's they were ready to close the grave suggesting they leave and come back when they were finished. They knew from experience it was always hard for the family to watch them cover their loved one with dirt. Jane refused to move. She wasn't ready to leave Tabitha.

When the grave was filled, Jane got up out of her seat and lay on top of Tabitha's grave. She needed to be as close to her as she possibly could. She couldn't force herself to let go. This is all she had left of her daughter and she wanted to hold on as long as she could.

Bill planned to follow the crowd back to the chapel where the service for little Judy Thornton would be starting shortly, but he couldn't leave his wife this way. He had a friend bring the car so he could take Jane home later when she was ready to leave.

Meanwhile, at the funeral home, the memorial service was starting for Judy Madison Thornton. She had such a small casket. It seemed absolutely forbidden that a body so small should be drained of its life, but the little girl was gone. Her life was over and her parents would have to find a way to cope with her loss.

Reverend Robert McClain would be doing her eulogy. He had known the family for many years. He could remember when Judy was born and how happy her parents were the day they brought her home. This never got easier. Pastor McClain had performed many funeral ceremonies and each one was heart wrenching. It was all he could do to get through them. Often times, he would find himself crying along with the families of the deceased.

Much the same group, who had attended Tabitha's ceremony, was in attendance for Judy's. Once again sadness overwhelmed the congregation. They were so sorry for the young parents who were here to mourn for their daughter. Daniel and Rosy Thornton were beside themselves with grief. They didn't know how to do this. What did everyone expect from them?

Reverend McClain began the eulogy.

"I stand before you today on this sad occasion to try and say goodbye to Judy Madison Thornton. She lived only a few short years, but left many wonderful impressions on everyone around her, especially her parents, Daniel and Rosy Thornton. I wish I knew what to say, but I know there are no words that can be said to ease your pain. This is by far the hardest thing you will ever attempt to conquer in life. It's never easy when we are forced to let go of a loved one, especially our own child, and even more so one so young and innocent. I know we wish Judy could stay with us, but she can't, and she is in a much better place now. She is in a place where no more harm can ever

59

come to her. *She's happy and playing. If she could, I know she would tell us how joyful her new home is. The family has asked me to read a poem for their little girl, written by her mother.*"

"*Your innocent smile and your beautiful face*
They warmed my lonely heart.
I thought for sure this day would never come, forcing your depart.
I'll hold your memory deep inside and guard it with my life.
Until I see you again my baby girl, on that you can rely."

The time had come for one last view of their daughter, and they weren't prepared for this. Was there anything that could prepare someone for something like this? If there was, the Thornton's hadn't found it. They were completely disgusted and consumed with misery, as their little girl would no longer be with them.

The usher motioned Daniel and Rosy to their daughter's casket. They rose and slowly walked to the front. They knew this walk meant their child was gone forever and they walked slowly, not ready to let her go. There must be some mistake. This couldn't be Judy. There must be some other child in town who closely resembles her.

"Oh Daniel, look at our sweet sweet girl. She looks like she is just sleeping. I think she may be breathing! They made a terrible mistake, Judy is still alive! Someone get our daughter out of here! She's not dead! She's breathing! She's alive!" Rosy began to scream.

It was all Daniel could do to take his wife out of the chapel and lead her to the car that would take them to Judy's grave. They had to follow behind the hearse. They could see their daughter in their imagination during the short drive. She always hated the dark, and now she was closed up in a box where there was nothing but darkness.

The Thornton's decided they would go home and come back to their daughter's grave at a later time. They didn't want to see the dirt as it covered her up. They just couldn't bear it. Judy was beneath the ground and she wasn't coming home; she was never coming home ever again. This was her final resting place.

The Thornton's knew they would eventually have to find a way to go on without Judy, but today was not the day. All they wanted to do was go back to the way everything was before this horrible event claimed the life of their child. They wanted everything to return to normal.

Chapter Eight

The hardest part of a funeral is when it ends and you go home. That is when you start to notice the little things you always took for granted. Something as simple as setting one less plate and glass on the table for dinner, or being able to keep up with the laundry because there's not as much of it anymore. The certain things you would ordinarily buy at the grocery store, especially for that loved one who was no longer with you, when they are the only one who had that preference.

So many things change when you lose a member of your family, especially one of your children. Where do you go from that point? Just trying to find a new normal way of doing things is a total mystery in itself. How do you go forward when you feel like you've just been robbed of the past several years of your life? People always want to tell you that it gets better and time will heal all wounds, but most of the time each passing day seems to bring more emptiness into your heart.

Bill and Jane Sealy arrived at their home and noted it seemed so lonely. The house seemed to be so much larger now than it was before their daughter's death. Everything was exactly as they had left it, except the fact that Tabitha was nowhere to be found. So many memories were made between those walls. They lived in this very house when Tabitha Elaine Sealy was born; she had always been there. Tabitha was the life of the house and now she was gone.

Jane went to her daughter's bedroom in search of anything with a remote trace of her left in it. She had to find a connection to Tabitha. She felt as if all ties had been cut at once and it was killing her inside. Relief was nowhere in sight for Jane.

Lying on Tabitha's bed were the clothes she took off and changed the night she died. They still possessed the smell of her perfume. Jane picked them up and she held them to her face. She was longing to absorb the fragrance Tabitha left behind, and she began to scream. Bill was frightened by Jane's sudden outburst and ran to check on her.

When he got to the door of Tabitha's bedroom, he could see Jane holding Tabitha's shirt to her face. He realized quickly what was so upsetting for his wife. It was the faint trace of their daughter that would soon fade away. They couldn't even begin to imagine happiness in their lives again. A part of them died with Tabitha and they would never be able to get that part of themselves back again.

"Jane, are you okay?" Bill asked.

"No! I will never be okay again! Why does everyone keep asking me that? Does anyone understand how I feel? I just lost my baby girl! She's dead! She won't ever be coming home!"

"Don't you think I know what you have lost? She was my daughter too you know. I miss her too! My life is upside down the same as yours! I want my baby back too, but she's gone and there is nothing I can do to change that! I would give anything if time would roll back and I could change this, but I can't. I love you Jane and we have to get through this together. We will never rise above this alone."

Jane suddenly realized how selfish she was being, after all, Bill had lost something very special to him as she had. Tabitha was Bill's daughter too. Jane embraced her husband and they begin to cry on each other's shoulders.

"I am so sorry Bill! I know you loved Tabitha as much as I did. I haven't even stopped to consider your pain and suffering. We will rely on each other to make it through this. We will get through this Bill, we will, we have to. Tabitha would want us to find a way to go on, and that's why we're going to work really hard to do just that."

"I love you Jane. I miss Tabitha something fierce. We've lost so much already and I just can't stand the thought of losing anymore, especially not you. Please promise me that you won't ever stop loving me Jane. Promise me that you won't ever leave me, no matter what," Bill made his wife promise.

"I promise you Bill. I will always love you and I'm not ever going anywhere without you. You're all I have left. I just don't know if I can stand to keep living in this house. It's too hard. Everywhere I look I see or hear Tabitha, but she's not there."

"Honey, do you remember a while back when I got that job offer in Florida? That job is still open. We could put the house up for sale and go. The main reason we didn't want to go in the first place is because we didn't want to relocate Tabitha with her school and everything. It's different now, we can get away from this place and try to make a new life for ourselves and just start fresh. What do you think, Jane?"

Jane agreed with Bill that a fresh start would be a great idea, so he immediately called his boss and informed him of his decision to take the new job offer. He told Bill he would set everything up and would let him know when everything was in place. Arlen, his boss, anticipated the job would be settled and ready to take over in the next two weeks.

Jane decided to call the realtor tomorrow and put their house on the market. They had enough money saved to buy a new house in Florida. They could afford to make the move before this house was sold.

Suddenly the phone rang and Bill answered it. It was Officer Mack Johnson. He had some information they needed to be aware of.

"Hello?" Bill answered.

"Hello, Mr. Sealy, this is Officer Mack Johnson. I have some news for you, unfortunately not so good."

"What is it Officer? Did you find out what caused the car to malfunction?"

"Yes we did, and unfortunately it was no accident at all."

"So what are you saying? Do you mean to tell me that my little girl was killed on purpose?" Bill asked.

"I'm afraid so, Bill. One of the employees who was fired for failing a drug test decided he would take his revenge out on the fair owner by sabotaging the new ride. He removed part of the cable from the car that Randy and your daughter were riding in. That's what caused it to jump off of the track. The man responsible is also dead. When I went to his house to question him, he fled on foot running into the street and was hit and killed by a car. We found a piece of cable on him that we suspected he removed from the cars. It came back as a match to the other cables and was definitely part of the cable removed from the car."

"How could someone do something like that? Didn't he know kids were going to be on that ride, and the possibility of one of them dying was very real? Our daughter is dead because some drug addict got mad because he lost his job! I can't believe this. This is even worse than an unexplained accident. Our daughter was killed! She was murdered!" Bill raged.

"I'm very sorry Mr. Sealy. I just wanted to call you myself and let you know what happened before you heard it from anyone else."

"Thank you officer. I will talk to my wife."

When Bill hung up the phone he was outraged with anger. He couldn't believe that someone could be so selfish and uncaring. He picked up an ash tray and threw it at the wall. He raked his arm across the counter smashing everything in his path. He was so mad and upset, he didn't know what to do.

"Bill, what's wrong with you? Why are you breaking everything? Tell me what's wrong with you, right now!" Jane screamed at her husband.

"That was the detective working the case at the fair. Someone killed Tabitha on purpose! It was no accident; he did it on purpose! Why would someone do that, Jane? Why?" Bill asked.

"Oh my God, someone killed our little girl! Who did it? Where is he?" Jane questioned.

"He is dead. He was hit by a car and killed, during a chase with the police. I'm glad he is dead; only wish I could have killed him myself! This whole thing was completely unnecessary!" Bill shouted.

"That's it! As soon as we list the house on the market, we're taking our things and we're going to leave as soon as possible! I don't want to be here one second longer than we absolutely have to!" Jane screamed.

The Sealy's definitely couldn't stay here now. It was hard enough to be constantly reminded of their daughter's death by her absence. They knew they would never be able to bear the heartache of passing the fairgrounds time and time again with the knowledge that Tabitha's life had been cut short, simply because someone was angry and wanted vengeance.

✐ Chapter Nine ✐

*C*armen Martin decided to stay on for a few weeks with Daniel and Rosy. She would do the housework and cook so her daughter could just take it easy. Judy's death had really stressed Rosy out, and Carmen was worried about her pregnancy. She didn't want her to have any complications with the new baby. She was very concerned. She knew what Judy meant to her and knew her death was putting a lot of strain on her daughter.

Daniel's mom would be leaving later this afternoon to return home so she could go to work tomorrow. Jenny Thornton felt quite comfortable with the fact that Carmen would still be with the kids and knew she would take good care of them. She really didn't want to go home, but she had to return to work. She lived from paycheck to paycheck and she absolutely couldn't afford to miss one.

Exhausted, Daniel and Rosy laid down for a while. They hadn't had much rest since all of this began. They probably wouldn't get much now either, but they decided to try. They snuggled close together in need of comfort and solace.

Carmen began to prepare dinner for Daniel and Rosy as they had eaten little since the accident. She put a lot of time in to preparing a home cooked meal hoping it would raise their interest in eating. Daniel and Rosy loved her meatloaf, so she decided it would be the perfect choice. She prepared all of the fixings to go with it and made a gallon of tea.

Carmen was setting the table and in another fifteen minutes dinner would be ready. When she filled the glasses with ice, she went to wake Daniel and Rosy.

"Hey guys, get up! Dinner is ready; come and eat," Carmen called.

When Rosy stood up from the bed, she was horrified at what she saw. On the bed where she was lying was a blood-stain on the sheet. She still had two months to go in her pregnancy. This couldn't be happening! Could she be losing the unborn child that she carried inside? She just said goodbye to one child; surely she wasn't about to bid farewell to another one!

"Daniel, look at the bed where I was laying!" Rosy shouted.

"Oh my God, we have to get you to the hospital now! Grab your jacket and let's go Rosy!" Daniel yelled.

They rushed quickly to get Rosy to the hospital as soon as possible. They were flabbergasted! Could this really be possible? Daniel and Rosy were not willing to calmly accept another loss; they were determined to make it to the emergency room before it was too late!

"You go and get the car, and I will help Rosy to the door! Hurry up!" Carmen demanded.

Daniel started the car and went back to the house to get Rosy who was now waiting at the front door. If he had to, he would carry her. Carmen had some lose ends to tie up before she could leave for the hospital. As soon as she finished, she would go straight to the emergency room.

Daniel had his wife loaded into the car and within minutes they were on their way to Tanner Medical Center.

As Carmen gathered her purse and started for the front door, the phone rang. She ran to answer it thinking it may be Daniel calling about Rosy.

"Hello?" she answered.

"Is Daniel or Rosy there please? This is Officer Mack Johnson. It's very important that I speak with one of them."

"I'm sorry sir, they're not here. Rosy just left for the hospital; she was having some complication with her pregnancy," Carmen explained.

"May I ask who I am speaking with ma'am?"

"I am Carmen Martin, Rosy's mother. Can I help you somehow?"

"I was calling to share the latest development in the case of their daughter's death. The car didn't leave the track by accident. The cable holding it on was tampered with resulting in the runaway car."

"Are you serious? Someone tampered with the cable holding the cars on the track?" Carmen asked.

"Yes ma'am I'm afraid so. The young man responsible is also dead. He led me on a foot chase, ran in front of one our cruiser's and was killed at the scene. We found the piece of cable that he removed from the roller coaster in his pocket. That's what caused the terrible tragedy that claimed the girl's lives."

"This is terrible! Do you know why he would do such an unspeakable act?"

"He worked at the fair and failed a drug test causing them to fire him. He was angry and decided to get revenge by tampering with the cars. Would you please pass this information on to Daniel and Rosy, and tell them if they need to know anything else they can call me? Please tell them I am very sorry."

"Thank you, officer. I will let them know. Thanks, again."

Carmen was stunned by the information the officer just told her. Her granddaughter was dead because some sorry low down drug addict was mad he lost his job. She couldn't believe that someone was capable of something so unfeeling and cold. Judy died for something she had nothing to do with! How could this happen?

Carmen needed to take a moment to pull herself together before she could go to the hospital. She wanted to get to Rosy as quickly as possible, but this latest news severely upset her. She was overcome with a whole new level of horror. It was hard enough when there was no explanation of the events at the fair, but now the truth was even harder to deal with.

Carmen had no idea how she was going to tell Daniel and Rosy the news. She could only imagine what their reaction would be, but knew it wouldn't be good. They were already hurt to the very core, but now they would have the mixed emotions of hurt and anger. She had no doubt Daniel would be very angry when he learned the news. Carmen just hoped his anger wouldn't completely destroy him.

Carmen decided to call Daniel's mother before she heard the news from someone else. She knew she would be very upset, but even more so if it came as a surprise from someone else.

"Jenny? This is Carmen."

"Carmen, is everything okay with the kids?"

"Rosy had to go to the hospital because she was bleeding. The reason I called is to share some information from Officer Johnson. He gave me some very disturbing information."

"What is it Carmen? Tell me," Jenny insisted.

"The train that the kids were riding in at the fair did not leave the track by accident. Some kid working at the fair failed a drug test, was fired and decided to get revenge by taking a piece of cable connecting the cars together," Carmen told her.

"Are you kidding me? You mean to tell me that our precious grandbaby is dead because some little punk got mad at the owner? Who did it?" Jenny asked.

"The officer didn't give the name, but he did say he had been killed when the police tried to question him. He was struck by a police car while attempting to escape," Carmen explained.

"Good, I'm glad he's dead! He doesn't deserve to live. Why would someone do something like this? This is unbelievable! Unbelievable!" Jenny responded.

"I am on my way to the hospital now, I haven't told the kids yet. I will let you know when I have some information about Rosy and her pregnancy. I'll talk to you later dear."

"Okay. Thank you very much for calling me and letting me know what was going on. If you guys need me, just call. It doesn't matter what time it is, when you have some more information please call anyway. I'll talk to you later," Jenny said.

Jenny hung the phone up and dropped onto her couch. She was beside herself with grief and disgust. Did this man have a conscious, or was he born without one? Sweet little Judy was gone and there was someone to blame for it. It would have been easier to take if it was just an unexplainable freak accident. At least then there would have been nothing anyone could have done to prevent it, but this, this just wasn't acceptable.

Carmen arrived at the hospital and parked her car as close as she could to the front doors. She was still wondering how she was going to tell her daughter and son-in-law the news from the officers phone call. She knew she needed to find some way to break it to them gently but didn't know how.

When she entered she saw Daniel at the nurse's desk filling out some paperwork. He was by himself. She didn't see Rosy so she assumed they had already taken her for treatment. She asked Daniel to step outside so she could tell him the information from the officer.

"Is something wrong Carmen?" Daniel asked.

"It's not good news, that's for sure. I will tell you outside."

Daniel finished the papers and stepped outside with Carmen. He was eager to find out what was so pressing and private. He wasn't ready for the words he was about to hear.

"When I was getting ready to come to the hospital, Officer Johnson phoned. He asked me to pass along some news to you and Rosy. I don't know how to tell you this," Carmen started.

"Just spit it out Carmen. Tell me what's going on," Daniel insisted.

"They solved the case. The car didn't accidentally leave the track. She then repeated the entire story as told to her by the officer.

"Please tell me you're wrong! Someone murdered my little girl! This has to be some kind of mistake. No one could be that heartless and cruel! There's no way that someone would do that on purpose, not when they knew kids would be on the rides. Why would they do that? Who did it?" Daniel asked.

"Officer Johnson didn't tell me the name. He said he was killed during a foot chase with the police. The detective asked me to let you know if you had any further questions you were more than welcome to call him."

"I can't believe this! Our little girl is dead and there is no excuse for it! Some idiot killed my kid, simply because he lost his job. Why didn't he vent his anger some other way? Why did he have to do this? Oh my God! My poor baby, she died for no reason! Her death was totally uncalled for!" Daniel shouted.

"I know—I was utterly astounded myself. I could have lived with an accident that no one could explain better than this," Carmen shared.

"It's a good thing this dude is dead! I swear I would have killed him if I could have got my hands on him. We can't tell Rosy about this yet. Let's wait until they're finished examining her. We need to tell her soon before she hears it in the news, and I don't want her to find out that way. We'll tell her as soon as we return home."

They both agreed this was the best way to handle the situation. The first priority was to keep Rosy calm until they found out what was wrong with her. Hopefully the doctors would be able to determine the cause of her bleeding and provide treatment. Daniel and Rosy needed everything to be alright with this baby. They needed a reason to keep going, and the baby was that reason.

After being examined for several hours and after a battery of tests including a sonogram, the doctors determined the baby was healthy and doing well. They believed the bleeding was caused by stress and Rosy being overly active. They recommended bed rest for the duration of the pregnancy. The doctor also gave them the good news, their baby was a little girl.

Carmen volunteered to stay with her daughter until the pregnancy was full term. She was willing to do whatever was necessary to insure the healthy birth of her grandchild. She was anticipating her arrival more now than ever.

"We're having a girl Daniel! Can you believe it? I already know what I want to name her. I think we should call her, Samantha Marie," Rosy excitedly shared with her husband.

❧

Daniel pulled the car to the front door, and he and Rosy started on the drive home. It was straight to bed for her when they arrived.

Daniel held his thoughts on the drive home. He was overflowing with frustration and rage, but knew he had to be as calm as possible for his wife's sake. He didn't want to upset her any more than she already was. The information from the officer was going to be risky for his wife's condition, but he had no choice except to tell her. If he didn't someone else would. He just couldn't take a chance on that. She needed to hear it from him.

When Rosy was settled in at home, Daniel decided to break the news to her. He knew she wasn't going to take this well at all.

"Rosy, I have something to tell you, and I warn you, you need to brace yourself. I dislike telling you, but if I don't, you'll find out some other way."

"What is it Daniel?"

"The detective on the case at the fair called here tonight. They have closed the case. They know what caused the car to jump the track," Daniel continued.

"What was it Daniel? Go on."

"Some guy who was fired for failing a drug test got mad, and decided it would be a smart idea to remove part of the cable holding the cars together. He did it for revenge. Judy's death was no mishap; the jerk did it on purpose."

"Oh no, there has to be some other explanation for this, otherwise Judy was killed on purpose. Her death could have been prevented. Could someone really do that? Why would they do that? They wanted someone to die! Oh my God! Daniel, someone murdered our child! Do they know who did it?" Rosy asked.

"Yes, but he was killed too. He led police on a foot chase and during his attempt to escape he was hit by one of their cruiser's. He was killed instantly," Daniel assured her.

"This is awful! Judy had nothing to do with this idiot being fired, and yet she paid the price. He shouldn't have used the drugs and then he wouldn't have failed the test. He would still have a job and my baby would still be alive. This is crazy! I'm glad he's dead! He doesn't deserve to draw another breath because none of his victims will ever be able to," Rosy expressed.

After hearing all the details, Rosy became very emotional. How could someone kill those kids? He claimed the life of those girls because he couldn't work at the fair anymore, and in the end it even cost him his own life. There's no way this was even remotely worth it. This young man's anger completely rearranged a number of lives. He stole the whole town's peace of mind. It will be hard for anyone to ever trust the rides at the fair again.

After several hours, Rosy finally cried herself to sleep. It hurt so bad realizing their daughter didn't have to die. Why didn't that man find another way to release his frustration? He had to know that someone would at least be badly hurt, and yet he was still willing to take the chance. The price for his madness was exceptionally high.

✍ *Chapter Ten* ✍

*I*t had been a while or so it seemed, since James and Megan were able to spend any time together. They made plans to go to the drive-in and see a movie. They didn't invite anyone else; they wanted to be alone.

With everything that happened in the past week or so, they now realized they definitely couldn't take each other for granted. The incident at the county fair put quite a few things in perspective for a lot of people, especially the kids in the town.

Most young people have a tendency to go through life with the idea that they are invincible and they will live forever. They have no thought of sudden destruction. The fairs events cleared that point of view up for the kids at Haralson County High. They lost two dear friends, and another was still in the hospital fighting for his life.

There was a new movie playing that Megan and James really wanted to see. It was filmed in Cedartown and they were anxious to see it. The name of it was Jayne Mansfield's Car. There were some really great actors starring in the movie; Robert Duvall, Billy Bob Thornton, and Kevin Bacon just to name a few. The thought of recognition for their small town in a movie was totally exciting for the youngsters.

Megan and James headed for the concession stand to get some snacks. They walked hand in hand to the booth.

"I love you James," Megan expressed.

"I love you too, Megan."

Megan and James took their snacks, returned to their car and settled in to watch the movie. Megan slid close to James which prompted him to put his arm around her. He squeezed her tightly to him.

James started kissing Megan. At first he kissed her softly on her lips, but then he pressed his lips to hers with more force and aggression. She could tell James was letting himself get more carried away than he should allow. She wasn't too worried until he placed his hand on the curve of her breast. She started to freak out then. She pushed him away and strongly expressed her dis-approval.

"Stop James, don't do that! I told you I wasn't ready for this! I'm scared. I don't want to get pregnant. I don't want to do this!" Megan firmly stated.

"Why not Megan, don't you love me? If you love me then you'll do it!" James pressured.

"I do love you, you know I do, but I'm not ready for this. You promised me you would wait until I was ready."

"I don't want to wait anymore! I want to make love to you."

"Take me home James. I can't believe you're behaving this way. You know I love you and you say that you love me too, but you are trying to use my feelings against me just to get what you want. How can you do this to me?"

"What if something happens to one of us the way it did to Randy and Tabitha? What if we don't have another chance to be together? Why should we waste time that we aren't guaranteed?" James pleaded.

"I don't believe you James Jackson! You are honestly using Randy's and Tabitha's misfortune to persuade me to sleep with you! You should be ashamed of yourself! I said take me home, now!"

James started the car and raced the engine. He was frustrated and angry with her for her rejection. He was tired of this. He wasn't going to be turned away any longer. If Megan wouldn't give in to his needs, then he would just have to find someone who would.

The drive home was in silence. Neither James nor Megan spoke a single word on the way home. Megan put her head up against the window and began to cry. She couldn't believe James was this adamant and pushy. This wasn't the way you treated someone you loved. She could never do this to him.

As the car approached Megan's drive, she gathered her things together and got ready to get out. She needed to delay going inside her house so her mother wouldn't know she was crying. If she knew, her mother would insist on knowing why, and Megan didn't want to share that information. She would handle this problem on her own.

Fortunately, her mother was already in bed and fast asleep. This would save Megan a lot of explaining. She went straight to her room and threw herself across her bed. She buried her face into her pillow and used it to muffle the sounds of her moaning. She was so hurt and upset. She never thought she would see the day when James would be so insensitive and selfish.

Megan noticed her phone showed a text message from James. What more could he want to say to her tonight. When she opened the message it upset her even more, as

James wanted to break up with her. Why was he taking this so far? She didn't want to lose him and he knew it. Was he trying to wear her down? That had to be it! He didn't really want to break up with her either, or at least she hoped he didn't.

Megan desperately needed to talk to someone, and since Tara was her best friend, it had to be her. She decided to give her a call, but not give her the details; she would just tell her that she and James had an argument and he wanted to break up with her.

"Hello?" Tara answered.

"Hey, what were you doing?" Megan asked.

"I was reading a book. What are you doing?"

"James just sent me a text message telling me that he wants to break up with me. We had an argument tonight, and now he doesn't want to be with me anymore," Megan explained.

"Are you serious? What happened?"

"I can't really tell you what the argument was about. I just need you to see if James will talk to you. Maybe you can talk some sense into him. I've already tried and he's not budging for me," Megan told her friend.

"Okay, I'll try. He may not talk to me either but I'll give it a shot anyway. I'll call you back in a minute."

Tara was puzzled by Megan's phone call. She wouldn't tell her what they argued about. How was she supposed to talk some sense into her brother when she wasn't even aware what the problem was? This wasn't going to be easy but she promised Megan she would try.

Tara went to James' room and knocked on the door.

"Come in!" James invited.

"What happened between you and Megan tonight?" she asked.

"What did she tell you?" James fished.

"She wouldn't tell me anything except that you sent her a text message telling her you wanted to break up. Why don't you tell me what happened?"

"I don't want to talk about it. I just think it would be best if me and Megan weren't together anymore. I'm ready to move on. I'll be leaving soon, anyway, so what's the big deal?"

"The big deal is that Megan loves you and she doesn't want to break up," Tara told him.

"Too bad, you don't always get what you want; she should know that by now, I do."

"That's the best you can do, James?" Tara asked.

"This conversation is over. Tell Megan I don't want to see her anymore. It's over."

Tara left her brother's room even more confused than when she entered it. What in the world could have happened between these two that would cause this? Tara didn't know what to think, but if James and Megan were unwilling to tell her, then there was nothing more she could do.

"Hello?" Megan answered.

"He's not telling me anything except he doesn't want to be with you anymore. What happened Megan? I can't help you guys if you don't tell me what is going on," Tara said.

"I'm sorry Tara, I just can't tell you what this is about. I wish I could but I can't."

"Well, then there's nothing I can do. Maybe he'll feel differently in the morning. I hope so," Tara said optimistically.

"Thanks anyway for trying. I'll talk to you in the morning. I love you!" Megan said.

"I love you too, good-night."

Maybe Tara was right. Perhaps James would feel differently after a good night's sleep. She sure hoped so. She couldn't bear the thought of losing him. She would have to rethink her position before she allowed that to happen.

✎ Chapter Eleven ✎

*B*lake Barker had just arrived at Grady Hospital to be with Randy and Jessica. He replayed the funerals over and over in his head, and continued to pray that he and his wife wouldn't face those same circumstances. Things weren't looking good for his son as Randy was constantly battling one setback after another.

Just as he opened his door to get out of his car, his phone rang. He didn't recognize the number, but decided to answer it anyway. It might be from the hospital with some news about Randy.

"Hello?" Blake answered.

"Is this Mr. Barker?" the voice asked.

"This is Blake Barker, can I help you?"

"Mr. Barker, this is Officer Mack Johnson, the detective handling the case at the fair. I have some news for you concerning the accident."

"Did you find the cause of the accident?" Blake questioned.

"Unfortunately we did sir, and the reason is not good. The ride was tampered with by a disgruntled former employee." The officer continued to tell him everything that happened.

"Why would someone do something that underhanded and cruel?"

"I don't know Mr. Barker, and I am sorry to have to give you the news, but I wanted you to hear it from me first; I felt like that would be the least I could do."

"I can't believe this! That name sounds very familiar for some reason too. I know that name from somewhere. This is ridiculous! I appreciate your calling me and letting me know. I will tell my wife. She's going to be horrified. Thank you, very much," Blake said.

"If either you or your wife has any questions at all, please feel free to call me. I will do my best to answer them for you. Good night, sir."

Blake couldn't grasp the story from the detective. His son was lying in a hospital bed fighting for his life because some jackass was angry with their boss for firing them. This was horrific! What did that little punk think he would accomplish? That's the good of drugs! How was he supposed to make his wife understand this nonsense? This situation continued to become more and more unbelievable.

He was contemplating the best way to break the news to Jessica believing she would not take it well. It was very difficult to accept the fact that something horrible happened to their son, but now to find out that it happened because someone wanted it to happen, was exceptionally hard to grip. What's wrong with people in this world today? Does human life have no value anymore?

As Blake exited the elevator, he saw his wife at the vending machine getting a soda. He figured now was as good time as any to break the news.

"Jessica, I'm glad I caught you alone. There is something I need to tell you. Brace yourself!" Blake warned.

"What is it Blake? What's wrong?"

"Officer Johnson called a few moments ago. They know what caused the accident," Blake said.

"What caused it?" she asked.

He then told her the entire story he learned from the detective.

"That can't be true! There's no way that someone would purposely do something this awful! There must be some misunderstanding," Jessica hoped.

"There's no misunderstanding Jessica, it's true. He did it on purpose. His name was Kirk Cannon. I know that name somewhere but I just can't place it. Does it sound familiar to you?"

"That was the kid who used to come to the house all the time and stay with Randy. He was the one with the braces. Are they sure it was him? He seemed like a good kid." Jessica said.

"Yes, they are sure. Now I remember, he's the one who lived on College Street," Blake replied.

"That's terrible. So many lives have been changed, and for what? Drugs, that's what! Why can't these kids figure out how bad drugs are before they get so involved with them? If only they could see it before it's too late!" Jessica frustratingly stated.

Blake pulled Jessica close to him in an effort to calm her down. She was very upset with the news and just couldn't comprehend the thought of someone being so carelessly cruel and heartless. Not only did he take the lives of others and almost killed her son, he forfeited his own life for nothing.

"How has Randy been doing today? Has anything changed?" Blake asked, changing the subject.

"There hasn't been any change so far. I wish he would wake up. I hope he is able to get through this because I can't bear the thought of letting him go. I love him so much!" Jessica said.

As they walked back to the waiting room, they were met by Jackie Massey, Jessica's brother. He was running toward them. They were alarmed something awful happened with Randy and rushed down the hall to meet him.

"The doctor is looking for you. He said he needed to talk to you. He said it was good news. He wouldn't tell us what it was, just said that he needed to talk to you. He said to go to the nurse's station when you returned, and have you call him," Jackie blurted with excitement.

Blake and Jessica quickly picked up the pace eager to talk with the doctor and hear the good news. What could it be? They couldn't wait to find out.

When they arrived at the nurse's station they asked for Dr. Hardy. The nurse instructed them to have a seat and she would check with the doctor.

"Mr. and Mrs. Barker, I have some great news for you. Randy has awakened and he's asking for you. He doesn't know what happened and I'm not sure we should tell him yet. I don't know how well he will handle that news. Didn't you tell me his girlfriend was killed in this accident?" Dr. Hardy asked.

"Yes sir she was," Jessica informed him.

"I am not so sure it would be a good idea to break that horrible news to him now. Try to avoid answering any questions concerning the accident, or at least as much as you can. If he insists on knowing, have the nurse get me and I will help you tell him. You can go back and see him now if you wish," Dr. Hardy told them.

Jessica and Blake were ecstatic with the news the doctor gave them. Their son was awake and it meant he might make it after all. It was touch and go for quite a while, and they hadn't been so sure that he would pull through. Randy was alive. They dreaded telling him about Tabitha's death. They didn't know how he was going to react. They were together for a long time and deeply cared for each other.

When they entered Randy's room they couldn't believe it. He was awake for the first time in nearly a week. It was so good to see he had finally awakened.

"Hey baby, how are you feeling? It's great to see you are awake. You gave us quite a scare for a while. Can I get you anything? I love you Randy!" Jessica told her son.

"No Mom, I don't need anything. The only thing I want to know is what happened? Where is Tabitha? Is she coming later?" Randy asked his mom.

"The doctor said you are doing much better. I'm very relieved you're going to be okay." Jessica tried to elude her son's question about Tabitha.

"Mom, I asked you a question, answer me! Dad, where is Tabitha? I want to know right now! Somebody tell me the truth! Where is Tabitha?" Randy demanded.

Jessica left to have a nurse call the doctor. Randy was not going to give up until someone explained where Tabitha was, and he wanted to know now.

"Randy, the doctor will be here in a minute. He will answer any questions you have. Just hang on and I promise he will tell you everything," Jessica assured him.

The doctor arrived prepared to answer Randy's questions. He hoped the knowledge of his girlfriend's death wouldn't cause a setback in his condition.

"Randy how are you?" the doctor asked.

"I'm fine doctor. I want to know where Tabitha is and no one will tell me. Can you tell me doctor? Will you make someone tell me where she is?" Randy pleaded.

"I'm sorry to have to be the one to tell you Randy, but Tabitha was killed in the accident. She was buried today. I'm very sorry."

"No! You're lying to me! Why would you say that? I don't believe you! She can't be dead! She has to be okay!" Randy shouted.

"Randy, it's the truth son. Tabitha is gone. She was killed instantly. She's gone! I'm so sorry," Blake told his son.

"What happened, Dad?" Randy questioned.

"The car you two were riding in, left the track, flew through the air and hit the ground. Tabitha was killed on impact. There was nothing that anyone could do for her. I'm sorry." Blake explained.

"She didn't even want to ride but I talked her into it. It's my fault! I should have been the one to die, not her. Oh my God! I can't live without her! We were about to be married and start a life together. Why did this have to happen? Someone tell me why!" Randy yelled.

Blake went to the side of the bed and put his arms around his son. He held him as tightly as he could. He could feel him shaking all over. Randy was hurting so much. Their hearts were breaking for their son and they felt helpless. They didn't know what they could do to ease his pain. He loved Tabitha so much and the realization of her death was ripping him apart, and he was now blaming himself.

The doctor ordered the nurse to give Randy medication to calm him down. The shot worked immediately and he drifted off to sleep. His parents returned to the waiting room so he could rest. They felt so sorry for him. It was going to be a long way back to normalcy for Randy. He would probably never be the same again.

❧ Chapter Twelve ☙

The Sealy's managed to get their house listed, and were tying up all the loose ends in preparation for their move. They realized they hadn't talked to the Barker's since the tragedy of losing Tabitha. They loved Randy and were thankful he was alive, but they couldn't help but wish Tabitha would have been the one to escape death.

They received updates on Randy's condition from other people in the community, but they hadn't quite got up the nerve to go see him. They knew this was something they needed to do prior to leaving town in two days. They completed everything necessary for them to leave which allowed them some time to make the trip to see Randy.

When Bill and Jane arrived at the hospital, they parked a rather lengthy distance from the entrance. As they walked towards the entry doors, the closer they came, the bigger the lump in their throats seemed to be. They knew just the mere sight of Randy would bring back an insurmountable feeling of pain and sorrow.

When they reached Randy's room, they knocked on the door awaiting permission to enter. It came almost immediately.

"Randy how are you dear?" Jane asked.

"I'm fine health wise. How are you guys doing? Are you okay?"

"We're just taking it from day to day sweetheart. That's the only thing we know to do," Jane replied.

"We're selling our house and I am going to take a job offer in Florida. It was offered a while back, but I wasn't interested then. Jane and I now feel the move will do us some good."

"I sure do hate to see you two go. Are you sure you want to leave?" Randy asked.

"Yeah we're sure, we've thought it completely through and we feel it's best," Bill responded.

"I've really wanted to talk to you guys, but I haven't had a chance to call. Will you please forgive me?" Randy pleaded.

"What for, Randy?" Jane asked him.

"It's my fault that Tabitha is gone," Randy answered.

"How is it your fault?" Jane questioned.

"Tabitha didn't even want to ride the Jumble Jack, but I insisted she ride it anyway. She only got on that ride because I begged her to. I am so sorry! I should have left her alone. I had no right to push her into it! I'm sorry!" Randy sobbingly told them.

Jane walked over to Randy and hugged him. She felt so sorry for him.

"You mustn't blame yourself Randy, it wasn't your fault. You had no way of knowing what was going to happen. You just wanted to share your experience with her. It's not your fault. It's not," Jane said.

"But if I hadn't been so adamant about her riding, she wouldn't have died! I will never forgive myself! Do you know how much I loved Tabitha? I would have given my life for hers any day. Why didn't I get that choice? She would still be alive. I'm so sorry Mr. and Mrs. Sealy! I'm sorry!"

"Randy it wasn't your fault. You had nothing to do with her death. We know that you wouldn't have let her get on the ride if you knew beforehand what was going to happen, but you had no way of knowing. You weren't the one responsible. The one who tampered with the cable is the one to blame, not you. We know how much you loved her, and we also know that you would have done anything you could to prevent this, the same as we would, but there was nothing either of us could do to save her. It was meant to be. God needed her in heaven, so he called her home. It's hard enough to accept the fact that she's gone, so please don't blame yourself. You'll never be able to heal that way. We love you, and we'll miss you very much. We don't blame you for Tabitha's death and neither would she." Jane tried to comfort him.

Bill and Jane visited for a while longer and then decided it was time to leave. They wanted to get home before dark. They said their goodbyes and they were on their way.

"I am so sorry for Randy. We should have come to see him sooner. I didn't realize he was blaming himself for Tabitha's death. I hope he can put his feelings of guilt behind him and just start to innocently grieve for her loss. It's going to take him a long time to get over this. He's so young and tender. I couldn't imagine having to deal with something this horrible at his young age. It must be terrifying," Jane said.

"He is pitiful alright. I hope he can start to mend. I hate it that Tabitha's gone, but look at the survival issues

Randy now has to deal with. This is an absolute no win situation, either way," Bill said.

They drove in silence, each realizing Randy wasn't so lucky after all. The reality of the situation started to sink in. They knew their daughter would also have had a difficult time dealing with the guilt of surviving the accident if Randy was the one who had been killed.

As they pulled into their drive, they noticed a strange car parked at their home. They had no idea who it could be.

Hoping it was someone interested in their home, they walked over to the man and woman.

"Can we help you?" Bill asked.

"Yes sir. The realtor told us to come over and see if you would give us a tour of your house. We are interested in buying," the man told them.

"Sure we don't mind. I am Bill Sealy and this is my wife Jane."

"Nice to meet you sir, my name is Ronald Evans, and this is my wife Gina. These are our daughters Tricia and Addysan, and this is our youngest son, Parker."

"Nice to meet you, come this way. I hope you are pleased with the house. Make yourselves at home, and feel free to explore as you wish. If you need something just let me or Jane know and we'll be glad to help you. Take as much time as you need," Bill told the family.

Jane and Bill went outside on the porch so the Evans could have some privacy. If they bought the house, the Sealy's would be completely unattached to Felton which would be wonderfully convenient. That would leave them no reason to ever come back to this small town.

After thirty minutes or so the Evans came outside with smiles on their faces. They appeared to be satisfied with the tour.

"The house is absolutely gorgeous. We love it! It's a perfect size too. As of right now we definitely want it. We will meet with the realtor and complete the paperwork so we can get started. How is this neighborhood? Do you ever have any trouble?" Ronald inquired.

"It's a wonderful neighborhood. We've never had any problems with anyone. In fact, it's a rather close knit area. Everyone pretty much helps everyone out when they can, but they also keep to themselves. It's a good place to live, especially for raising children," Bill told them.

"Okay then, thank you very much for everything. We'll be in touch. Have a good day," Ronald said.

"You too Mr. Evans, we appreciate it. We're glad you like the house. It has served us well for over eighteen years. We'll see you!" Bill said.

The two men shook hands and the Evans returned to their car. They drove to town to begin the process of buying the house. They were very pleased with the house, and everything about it was lovely as far as they were concerned.

"That was quick, huh?" Jane asked her husband.

"No kidding, that must be a record for house marketing. I've never known of one selling that quickly before. It sure is good for us though, because now we can wrap everything up and be done with it completely," Bill pointed out.

The kids in the neighborhood went back to school today. Everyone was sad and moping, mourning the loss of their friend. Tabitha was on the cheerleading squad with Megan and Tara. She was well known by everyone. Her spot on the team had to be replaced, so Tara and Megan scheduled auditions the following week to pick a new cheerleader.

Megan texted James' phone several times, but he hadn't replied. She couldn't understand why he was being so stubborn about everything. Didn't he understand she was just trying to look out for both of them? If Megan ended up pregnant it would complicate things for her and James. Why couldn't he see that?

Megan decided to ask Tara if she spoke with James today. Maybe he gave his sister a clearer view of his intentions.

"Have you talked to James today?" Megan asked Tara.

"I talked to him earlier, why?"

"I've been texting him all day and he hasn't returned any of my messages. Did he say anything to you about me?" Megan asked hopefully.

"No, he didn't say anything to me. I don't know what his problem is."

"I am getting very upset about this whole thing. I don't want to lose James. What am I going to do?" Megan asked.

"I don't know Megan. Neither one of you will tell me what the problem is, so I don't even know how to begin to help you. I'm in the dark, remember?"

"If I tell you, do you promise not to say anything to James?" Megan made her swear.

"I promise, what is it?"

"James wants me to sleep with him. I tried to tell him I'm not ready to go that far and he got angry with me. I don't want to get pregnant. I know it would make things hard on both of us. He isn't interested in trying to understand my point of view; he just wants me to sleep with him," Megan explained.

"Are you kidding me? He broke up with you because you won't sleep with him?"

"That's what this whole thing is about. I didn't want to tell anyone, but James is taking this entire thing to the extreme. I don't know what to do," Megan said.

"I'm going to talk to him about this. He's being ridiculous!" Tara told her.

"You can't Tara! You promised! If he knows that I told you, he will never talk to me again," Megan pleaded.

"Okay Megan, I won't say anything, but how do you propose to work this out?"

"I don't know yet, hopefully I'll think of something," Megan told her.

Tara couldn't believe what Megan told her. Her own brother broke up with her just because she wouldn't give in and sleep with him. Tara loved James, but this didn't leave much respect for him. She was very disgusted and frustrated over this. She wanted to say something to him so bad but she promised Megan she wouldn't. He ought to be ashamed of his stinking self. Megan really cared for him, and he was taking advantage of that in the hope she would eventually give in to his desires.

The school planned a memorial service in memory of Tabitha which was scheduled for last period. The kids would be able to go home immediately following the service. The staff thought it to be better that way, since many of the students would probably be very upset. They were also taking up donations for the family, giving the kids a chance to do something important for Tabitha.

It was always extremely hard to deal with the loss of a loved one, especially one so young and full of life. No one is ever able to comprehend the significance of tragedy, especially school children with little life experience. They seemed to think that death was something in the future, ignoring the possibility of its early arrival.

The staff and children at Judy's school were struggling to accept her passing. It was more or less impossible to explain her death to the small children. They definitely had no idea how to sort the tragedy out; however, the staff gave it their utmost effort. They too, had taken up a donation for the family to offer their sympathy.

☙ *Chapter Thirteen* ❧

*T*oday's top story in The Cedartown Standard and the Beacon Gateway was the story of the tragedy at the fair. It gave full details explaining the outlandish actions of nineteen-year-old Kirk Cannon.

The news outraged the community. They never thought someone who once was a respected member of the community could be so cold and callused. That just goes to show, you never truly know the person who lives next door.

Tara was horrified when she read the article. This meant that Tabitha and Judy were murdered and she couldn't understand such an act. Another disturbing fact was her brother James, had once been close friends with Kirk Cannon who used to live in Felton. When he moved away, he and James just drifted apart.

"Did you read the paper?" Tara asked Megan.

"Yes I just finished it. Can you believe that? What about Kirk Cannon? I always thought he was a good guy," Megan told her.

"He was. I guess when he got into drugs it just changed him. There's no way that I would do drugs; they make you crazy and apparently turn you into someone who has no conscious too," Tara said.

"Have you called the Barkers recently to check on Randy?" Megan asked.

"No, but I am going to call them in a little bit though. I hope he's doing better."

"Yeah me too, I hope he will be able to come home before too long," Megan said.

Tara had to go to the store for her mom and then she was going to call Mrs. Barker and see how Randy was doing. She passed James on her way out of the driveway. He waved at her but she didn't bother to wave back. She was still totally disappointed in the situation he insisted on dragging out with Megan.

When James didn't see Tara wave at him, he wondered what was wrong with her. Had Megan told her what happened? He would message Megan and ask her.

Megan was doing her homework when she heard the tone indicating she had a message. She was excited at first, only to discover it was James who sent it.

"Did you say something to Tara about what was going on with you and me? If you did, you had no right. Don't try to turn my sister against me. It won't ever work, I promise you that. Blood is thicker than water, remember that." the text read.

She ignored his message and decided she would call Tara and make sure she hadn't said anything to James. She promised Megan that she wouldn't.

"Hello?" Tara answered.

"Did you say anything to James about what I told you today?" Megan asked.

"No, didn't I promise you I wouldn't? I didn't tell him anything."

"He just sent me a text and asked if I told you what was going on between us. I didn't answer it. He warned me that I better not be trying to turn you against him, since blood is thicker than water," Megan told her.

"He's crazy. I didn't tell him anything. He waved at me when he drove into the yard and I didn't wave back; that's probably why he asked. Don't worry about it," Tara said.

When Megan ended the call, Tara returned to the message James sent her on her phone. She started to reply, but changed her mind. If it ever came out she told Tara about all of this, she didn't want to lie to James about it. If she simply didn't reply, she wasn't lying.

Tara returned home from the store, and decided to call Jessica Barker and inquire about Randy.

"Mrs. Barker, this is Tara Jackson. I wanted to find out how Randy is doing."

"He's doing great Tara. He regained consciousness. He took the news about Tabitha pretty hard, but his health has improved tremendously. The doctors are hopeful for a speedy recovery. He should be coming home soon if everything continues to improve. They still say he won't ever walk again, but we're going to start therapy anyway," Jessica excitedly shared.

"That's great Mrs. Barker, I am so glad to hear that. I will let everyone else know too. I'm sure they will be as happy about it as I am. Will you please tell him I called? Tell him we miss him too!"

"I sure will Tara. Thanks for calling. Randy will be glad you did. I'll talk to you later dear."

"Thank you Mrs. Barker, see ya."

Tara was excited about the news, and it sounded as though Randy was going to be fine. She had been so worried about him, but now she could breathe a sigh of relief.

Tara heard the sound of an engine outside. She went to the window saw it was a moving van at the Sealy's old house. They hadn't been gone long and someone was already moving into it. She decided to go across the street and welcome them into the neighborhood.

"Hello, how are you folks? Do you need some help with anything?" Tara offered.

"No we're fine. Who are you?" Tricia, their daughter asked.

"My name is Tara Jackson, I live across the street. I knew the people who lived here real well. Their daughter was a good friend of mine. She was killed in an accident recently; I guess that's why Mr. and Mrs. Sealy decided to move."

"My name is Tricia. We just moved here from Rome. We wanted to move to a smaller town and this is where we landed. I hated to leave my old school though; I was the captain of the cheerleading squad."

"That's rather ironic. I am the captain of our cheerleading squad. We're doing auditions this week for an open position on the team if you are interested."

"Yeah, thanks for telling me. That's great." Tricia said.

"Tara, Mom wants you home right now!" James shouted from across the street.

"Who's that? He's cute." Tricia inquired.

"That's my older brother James."

"Well, I guess I better go before my mom gets angry with me. Nice to meet you Tricia, and don't forget about cheerleading auditions. They will be held every day after school. If you want to you can ride home with me," Tara said.

"Thanks I just may do that. I will speak with my mom and dad and see what they think. I'll let you know."

After dinner Tara decided to call Megan and update her on Randy's condition.

"Hey, what are you doing?" Tara asked.

"I just finished taking a shower, how about you? Did you call Randy's mom?"

"I sure did, that's what I was calling to tell you. He is doing much better. He regained consciousness. His mom said he may even get to go home soon. They still don't think he will be able to walk again, but they are starting therapy in hopes that he might," Tara explained.

"Good, I'm so glad for him. Who knows, he might beat the odds," Megan said.

"Did you notice the moving van next door at the Sealy's old house? They have a daughter who will be going to our school. She said she was the captain of the cheerleading squad at her old school. I told her we were doing auditions all this week after school. Maybe she will be able to fill the spot," Tara stated.

"That's good. Is she nice? Do you like her?" Megan inquired.

"She seems really nice. I think I will like her. You will probably like her too. You'll be able to meet her tomorrow. I offered her a ride home after school," Tara told her.

"Okay, I hope I like her. I probably will, if you do," Megan agreed.

Megan looked out the window trying to get another look at the new girl. What she saw led her to believe that the hope of liking her just faded. James was on her front lawn talking to her. They appeared to be flirting with each other. What did James think he was doing?

Megan and James were only broken up for a few days and he was already putting the moves on the new girl. Was he doing this to make her jealous, or was he truly ready to find someone else? There is no way Megan would stand idly by and let her boyfriend turn his affections to another girl. That just wasn't going to happen.

Megan called Tara.

"Tara, look out your window. Look at James; he's at the house next door trying to hook up with the new girl. What did you say her name is?" Megan asked.

"Her name is Tricia, hang on a minute and let me get to the window where I can see."

"Do you see him? He is being such a jerk! I feel like going out there and strangling him! He is making me very mad!" Megan expressed.

"She asked me who he was when he came outside to call me in for dinner, but I didn't say anything about you being his girlfriend. She doesn't know, but he does. Come over here and you can talk to him when he comes back," Tara told her.

"Okay, I'll be there in a minute," he said.

Megan hung up the phone and went to Tara's. She was going to settle this thing with James once and for all. This was very childish and she was tired of his game playing. She was being persuaded more and more into doing the unthinkable. She didn't want to sleep with James, but she definitely wasn't willing to set back and just let him go either.

When Megan arrived at the house, Tara told her to go to James' room and wait for him. Tara would text James and lie, telling him their mother said for him to get home. That way he wouldn't keep talking to Tricia.

A few moments later the door slammed as James came in. He had no idea Megan was waiting for him in his bedroom.

"What are you doing James?" Megan asked her former boyfriend.

"What do you mean, what am I doing?"

"Why were you flirting with Tricia? You just broke up with me two days ago James and you're already flirting with someone new. Why do you have to be this way?"

Megan was shaking all over. Her emotions were taking over. She was mad but was extremely heartbroken. She wasn't sure what approach was the best to use.

"I love you James and I thought that you loved me too, but apparently I was very wrong. I don't want us to continue to be apart. I want to be together."

She moved closer to James in an attempt to gain his affection. She touched her lips to his very softly and gently. At first he didn't respond, but he quickly became receptive. Megan and James continued to kiss passionately. Before they knew it, things had gone further than they ever had before.

It happened. Megan and James' naked bodies were lying horizontally parallel to each other in bed. Megan's birth control was the only protection they had used. James didn't use a condom because they were so lost in the moment. They had lost their virginity together.

"I can't believe we just did that. We made love, and it was quite nice too. You didn't use a condom, James," Megan stated.

"It's okay Megan, you are taking birth control. I promise you that everything will be okay. Don't tell Tara about this. She will make a big deal out of it," James pleaded.

Megan agreed this would be their secret. She really didn't want to tell anyone else for fear of what their reaction would be. She was afraid everyone would think she was easy, and she didn't want that reputation. She knew a girl at school who had sex with her boyfriend and when it became known, everyone started calling her a whore. Megan didn't want to be known for that kind of behavior.

Chapter Fourteen

The Evans rose bright and early in the morning. Gina needed to take her children and register them in their new schools. Tricia would be attending the high school, Addysan would be going to the middle school and Parker was in the third grade. They were all cooperative and anxious to go.

Tricia was hopeful the other kids would be as nice and friendly as Tara was. At least she already knew someone who attended the new school. James was nice too, not to mention he was very good looking. Tricia was hoping to make the cheerleading squad, knowing it would improve her chances to make new friends.

Ronald worked at a company in Rockmart for the last fifteen years and made a decent wage. Gina didn't work since she had three children at home who needed her attention. Although, Tricia was actually old enough to babysit her younger brother and sister, Gina had never felt comfortable with that idea. She didn't trust anyone to care for her kids.

Tricia was the first one to register for school, since she was in high school and it was harder to keep up with. If Gina registered her oldest daughter first then she wouldn't be as late for classes.

Tricia discussed the cheerleading squad with her parents and they agreed it would be a good idea. She would take Tara up on the ride home offer.

The registration process for Tricia's classes had gone smoothly and she was headed to her first class in no time. She was relieved.

"Hi my name is Tricia, I'm new here. I just moved here from Rome," Tricia shared with her teacher.

"Okay Tricia, have a seat. My name is Ms. Davenport. I will be your English teacher. Let me get you a book. I'll be right with you."

Exploring her surroundings, Tricia saw Tara sitting in the back of the room. She waved at her. She was pleased that she knew someone in her class already. When Ms. Davenport finished with her, she found a seat close to Tara's. This was a good start to an otherwise, extremely nervous day.

When class was over, Tara and Megan went to their lockers, which were located next to each other. This simplified spending the entire school day together. Since Tricia hadn't been able to purchase a locker yet, Tara offered her to share hers with her. Tricia accepted; she definitely didn't want to be stuck carrying a bunch of heavy books all day.

"This is Megan, my brother's girlfriend," Tara introduced.

She decided to take advantage of the introduction and let Tricia know that James was spoken for.

"Nice to meet you, I'm Tricia."

Someone came up behind Megan placing their hands over her eyes. She knew it had to be James. No one else would even try that, not successfully anyway. He gave her a kiss and put his arm around her. He walked her to her next class.

When James left, Tara questioned Megan about how to solve her problem with him. Megan was unsure how she should respond. She couldn't lie to Tara, but she promised James she wouldn't tell anyone.

"We just worked it out, that's all." Megan told her.

"That's not what I asked you Megan. I asked how you were able to work it out."

"We just did, I told you," Megan repeated.

"Megan, did you sleep with him? You did, didn't you? You slept with James." Tara probed.

"Tara I promised I wouldn't say anything. You can't let James know that you know. If he finds out you do, he will kill me," Megan cautioned.

"I guess. How was it? Did you like it?" Tara inquired.

"It was nice actually. It was very nice. I liked it. I may do it more often now. I am still taking my birth control so I don't have to worry about getting pregnant."

"You still better make James use a condom just to be sure. I would hate for you to end up pregnant. I can't believe you did it. Did it hurt at all?" Tara asked.

"No not really, I told you it was nice. That's all I am going to say."

Tara was still a virgin, and she planned to stay that way until she was married, or at least until she was much older anyway. Thank God, Jake hadn't tried to pressure her into having sex, because if he did, she would probably break up with him. The thought of having sex absolutely terrified her. She wasn't sure if it was the thought she might become pregnant, or the actual act of doing it. Nevertheless, it wasn't happening any time soon.

❧

The day breezed by for Tricia and now it was time to try her luck at the cheer leader audition. She kept her fingers crossed hoping she would claim the open spot. She had been a cheerleader since fourth grade, so she was pretty confident with her ability to stir up a crowd.

When Tricia entered the gym she was pleasantly surprised to see that no one else had come to audition. That automatically placed her in the spot if she was able to please Tara and Megan. She was quite sure it wouldn't be a problem.

"As you can see no one else showed up but you. If you can pass a few demonstrations you will be the newest member of the cheer squad," Tara told her.

"I'm ready. What do you need me to do?" Tricia anxiously asked.

"I need you to do a split. Then we will have you recite a cheer," Tara explained.

Tricia was able to zoom through the demonstrations with flying color. She did an outstanding job. Tara and Megan were very pleased with her performance. She was appointed to the Haralson County cheerleading squad. She was exceedingly happy to be accepted.

"Are you riding home with me this afternoon?" Tara asked.

"Yeah, if you don't mind."

"I don't mind. Megan will be riding with us too. Congratulations on making the team. I will get you a schedule tomorrow," Tara told her.

Tricia hit the front door bursting with excitement about her new position. She was officially part of the cheer team. She couldn't wait to share it with her mother and father. She knew they would be proud of her.

"I made it Mom! I made the team!" Tricia shouted.

"That's great Tricia. I'm proud of you, good job. I knew that you could do it."

"I have some homework to do, and tomorrow I'll need eight dollars for a locker. Don't let me forget," Tricia told her mother.

James and Megan made plans to go to the drive-in again. This time would be more enjoyable than before since things were different between them. Sex was no longer an issue. As long as she continued to take her birth control pills she didn't have anything to worry about. She made James keep a condom in his pocket so they would have double the protection.

Megan's mom called for her.

"What were you saying Mom? I couldn't hear you the first time."

"I said I have to work second and third shift tonight. I won't be home until after you leave for school in the morning. Make sure to set the security system and don't forget to set your alarm."

"Okay Mom, I'll be sure to do both. James and I have a date tonight, is that okay?"

"I'd rather you would postpone it since I have to work. I don't feel comfortable with you being out and me not at home."

"I'll call James and tell him. Maybe he'll understand," Megan said discouragingly.

Megan needed to call James right away and let him know she needed to cancel their date. She was hoping he wouldn't get mad at her. Suddenly a thought popped into Megan's head that offered a way around the situation. She would tell James to tell his parents he was going to spend the night with a friend, but he could really stay the night with her since her mom was working all night.

"Hey baby, what are you doing?" Megan asked James.

"I'm thinking about you and our date tonight."

"About our date tonight, there's been a slight change of plans." Megan told him.

"What do you mean, can't you go?"

"I can't; my mom is scheduled to work a double shift at the hospital and she doesn't want me to go out because she won't be home. I have an idea though. You can tell your folks you're going to spend the night with Tank, and you can spend the night with me instead. You will need to call Tank and let him know so he can back up your story if necessary."

"That's a good idea. I'll call him and let him know, and then I'll call you back." James jumped right on board with Megan's deceitful plan.

Megan was bubbling over with excitement. She hoped James would be able to work it out with Tank. A few moments later her phone rang.

"Hey, I got it worked out. I will go to Tank's house in a little while and then he will bring me to your house after dark so no one will see me coming in. Tank's mom and dad have to work tonight too, so they won't know I'm not there," James explained.

"It sounds good to me. So what time do you think you will be coming?"

"Probably between nine and nine-thirty, I'll see you then. I love you!"

"I love you too. I can't wait."

The night was set. James and Megan would spend their first night together. Both of them were anticipating going to sleep together and waking up the same way. Megan imagined that someday soon when they were married they would spend every night in each other's arms. She wanted to spend the rest of her life as Mrs. James Jackson, and her dream was starting to become more and more real.

The clock on the mantle in the living room read nine o'clock. Just then, Megan heard the roaring of a car engine in front of the house. Her mother had been gone for hours. Megan peeked out the window and it was James. He was already knocking on the door by the time she could get a good look at the car. She let him in and they immediately went to her bedroom. Megan needed to take a shower before she was ready to go to bed. James decided he would take one when Megan finished.

"Your turn, I'm through," Megan told James.

"Will you get me a towel please?" James asked.

"I already laid one on the shelf next to the shower."

While James was taking a shower, Megan decided to get into bed and wait for him. She slipped into one of her night shirts. She started reading the book "The Stand" by Stephen King. She loved to read his work and thought he was extraordinarily gifted with his imagination.

Shortly, James appeared in the doorway with a towel wrapped around him. He turned the light out and he got into bed with Megan. He pulled her close to him and they began to explore the shape of their bodies. Their passion rose extremely high in a matter of moments. Once again they expressed the depth of their love for each other.

Megan spent the remainder of the night with her head on James' chest. She felt secure and safe in his embrace. They set the clock for five a.m. so it would still be dark when James left the house. Although, her mom would still be working they needed to be careful not to be seen by any of the neighbors, especially not Angela or Dave Jackson.

James and Megan continued to appreciate each other's company throughout the evening and early morning. They were sleeping soundly when awakened by the alarm clock. It was time to get up and get started. James called Tank to pick him up. In a very short time Tank was in the drive waiting. Megan and James kissed each other goodbye very warmly and he left.

Megan decided to get ready for school since she was already up anyway. She knew she wouldn't want to get up if she allowed herself to go back to bed and fall asleep. She wasn't taking any chances.

Chapter Fifteen

*R*andy started therapy in the hope of regaining his ability to walk. His legs were becoming stronger and stronger. It was looking hopeful that he would beat the odds against him. He was praying for a miracle.

The nurse took him to the therapy room to do his walking exercises with the assistance of parallel bars. He had gained a tremendous amount of strength in his arms, since he had to rely on them to hold him up. He struggled each time he got up but he was determined to walk again.

"Are you ready Randy?" nurse Godfrey asked.

"I'm ready when you are.'," the nurse instructed.

As his mother watched, Randy grabbed the bar and lifted himself out of his chair. He was more determined today than ever before. He was ready to reclaim his independence. No more calling for someone every time he needed to get up. This had gone on long enough.

At first, his legs shook almost uncontrollably but then he was standing with a strength and confidence he hadn't known for quite a while. He was going to do this. All of a sudden, he let go of the bars and he took his first step alone. The nurse looked on at him in amazement. She couldn't believe it. He had just taken a step without having to depend on anything but himself and his own will.

"Oh my God I did it. Did you see that? I took a step on my own. I told you I was going to walk again. I told you. I knew that I would," Randy excitedly expressed.

"Randy you did it. You walked! I am so proud of you son! I knew you could do it. I just knew that you would," Jessica encouraged.

Jessica could feel the tears running down her face. This was a wonderful sight to witness. Her son was going to be able to walk again. Soon, he wouldn't need help to go anywhere he wanted. He was well on his way to a full recovery. Jessica called her husband to share the good news. He would be happy too.

"Blake, it's me Jessica. Guess what your son just did. You'll never believe it."

"What dear, what did he do? Tell me."

"He just took a step on his own! Our son walked without any help! He's on his way back Blake, Randy will walk again."

"Oh, that's wonderful Jessica, I am so glad that you called me. I will be there as soon as I get off work. I love you. Tell Randy that I am very proud of him."

"Okay dear, I'll tell him. I'll see you this afternoon. I love you," Jessica told him.

"I love you too. I'll see you in a bit."

Blake hung up the phone and just sat there silently. His son had taken a step on his own. The doctors had diagnosed him as a paraplegic but he was proving them wrong. He was going to walk again. Randy would be home and back to his old self before they knew it. Blake was ecstatic over the accomplishment his son had made.

The nurse helped Randy back into his chair and took him back to his room. Once she settled him in, she went to page the doctor and let him know about the latest development. They didn't expect that he would ever walk again at all, especially not this soon.

"Dr. Hardy, this is Jill Godfrey, I am taking care of Randy Barker today. We just returned from therapy. He took a step totally by himself with no assistance. I thought you would want me to immediately update you to his improvement."

"He took a step without assistance? That's amazing. I didn't expect him to ever regain the use of his legs, and this is extremely soon. Schedule him for a MRI this afternoon. I will reevaluate his spinal injury and see what it reveals. I'm very pleased with the information. Thank you very much for your promptness, nurse Godfrey," Dr. Hardy expressed.

The nurse returned to Randy's room and informed him he would be getting an MRI this afternoon. She told him the doctor was going to take another look at his spinal cord injury. They didn't know what was going on with him, except he was starting to fully recover. In fact, they were almost convinced he would never be capable of a full recovery from this type of injury.

Blake finished work and headed to the hospital to be with his wife and son. He was overwhelmed with happiness over his son's improvement. Maybe this meant he would be going home sooner than expected. When he entered Randy's room he was surprised to see only his wife sitting there. Where had Randy gone; he wasn't in his bed?

"Where's Randy?" Blake asked.

"He went to have an MRI. The doctor wants to take another look at his spine. They want to reassess and see if anything has changed," Jessica told him.

"Oh, good, I hope it's healed. That would be wonderful."

"I hope the damage is less than it was. That would give Randy a better chance of recovering," Jessica shared with her husband.

The nurse brought Randy back to his room after the MRI and he was ready to return to bed. He seemed so much more hopeful because of the step he made earlier. The nurse told them the doctor would be in to see them shortly after he read the MRI.

"How are you feeling sport?" Blake asked.

"I'm doing great, Dad. Did Mom tell you I took a step on my own earlier when I was taking therapy?"

"She most certainly did and I am very proud of you. I knew that your stubbornness would come in handy one day. This time it presented a positive result that you can be excited about."

"I told you guys I would walk again, and I am going to do it too."

"Keep up the good work son."

The doctor arrived with Randy's MRI results looking somewhat puzzled. With any luck, this was good news for the Barker's.

"Randy, how are you today?" Dr. Hardy asked.

"I'm good."

"I have your test results, and I wouldn't believe them if I didn't have them right here in front of me. There's not one trace of the spinal injury that your first test showed. It looks like you will make a complete recovery. I have no medical explanation to offer. If I had to tell you who's responsible for your healing, I would have to say it was God. The first test that we did showed extensive damage and now it doesn't even exist."

"Thank you so much Dr. Hardy. We have been praying through this whole ordeal, and I also believe God was the one who healed my son," Jessica responded.

"Reconsidering your case, I have decided to let you go home tomorrow. You will need to continue your therapy in outpatient sessions. Can you handle that? Does that sound okay to you guys?" Dr. Hardy asked.

"That sounds wonderful to me doctor. I'm ready to get out of here and go home. I would like to sleep in my own bed again; it's much more comfortable than this hospital bed," Randy said excitedly.

The Barker's were overflowing with excitement. They could finally take their son home. He was on his way to a complete recovery. Randy was looking forward to going home and seeing all of his friends too. He should be able to go back to school soon, and he could hardly wait. He would still make graduation after all.

Jessica decided to call some of Randy's friends and set up a surprise party for his homecoming. Since she knew Randy was okay and on his way home tomorrow, she let Blake stay the night with him at the hospital and she would go home, decorate and prepare for the party.

"Blake if you don't mind, I would like you to stay with Randy tonight so that I can go home. I will tidy the house up and make everything comfortable for his return."

"That's fine dear. I don't have to work tomorrow. I'll be glad to stay with him tonight; it'll do you some good to go home for a night, anyway."

Jessica never let on to her son about her plans to throw him a surprise party. She didn't even disclose her plans to Blake. She was afraid Randy might overhear her and she wanted the party to be a complete surprise. Jessica kissed her son and her husband and she told them goodbye.

She decided Tara and James Jackson would be the best ones to call about the party for Randy. They were close friends with her son and knew they would want to be a part of his surprise. She would have them spread the word, since they were more familiar with the rest of Randy's friends.

"Tara, this is Mrs. Barker. Randy is scheduled to come home from the hospital tomorrow and I wondered if you and James would like to help me plan a surprise party to celebrate his homecoming. I know that you know more of Randy's friends than I do, so I wondered if you would mind spreading the word for me."

"Sure Mrs. Barker, we'll be glad to help. I'm glad he is coming home. I know you guys are happy for sure. What did they tell him?" Tara questioned.

"The spinal cord injury is gone. There isn't the slightest trace of it; it's as if it never occurred. He took a step by himself today and he was thrilled about it," Jessica shared.

"Oh my God, that's wonderful Mrs. Barker. So everything is going to be okay, right? He's going to be able to walk again, isn't he?" Tara asked.

Tara was totally overwhelmed with happiness about Randy being able to walk again. She wanted to call Megan and give her the good news. She would also request her help in preparing for the party. She and Megan could help Mrs. Barker decorate and organize the house and they would let James and Jake spread the word.

"Megan, Randy is coming home from the hospital tomorrow. He is going to be able to walk again too. Mrs. Barker wants to have a surprise party for him and she needs us to help her set up for it. I will get James and Jake to contact everyone and let them know," Tara told her.

"That's great! I'll be glad to help, just let me know when you get ready to do it," Megan said.

Tara ended her phone call with Megan and then went to her brother's room to let him know his part in the preparation. She wanted to let him know what he needed to do so he could get started.

"James, I need you to do something. The Barker's are bringing Randy home tomorrow and his mother wants to have a surprise party for him. Megan and I are going to help her organize everything at the house and we need you to let everyone know."

"Okay, I'll call Jake and Tank and get them to help me. How is he doing?" James asked.

"He's doing great; he took a step on his own today. The doctor did a new MRI and the original injury to his spine isn't there anymore. He is going to be able to walk again."

"Thank God, I am so glad he is going to be okay. I'll get started spreading the word about the party," James told her.

Everything was set in motion; Randy will be coming home to a party he doesn't expect. All of his friends will be there to welcome him home. He will be pleasantly surprised to see them. He is well on to his way to getting his life back.

It was a relief to know something from the events at the fair turned out right. It would be much easier if it hadn't happened at all but since it did, it was a nice change to see some positive results at last. Maybe everyone would start to feel more at ease again.

Chapter Sixteen

The following morning the doctor came into Randy's room bright and early. He brought the papers for Blake to sign releasing Randy from the hospital. Blake was glad his family could finally put this whole thing as far behind them as possible and try to get a fresh start.

Everyone knew it would take Randy quite a while to get over Tabitha's loss, but hopefully his own situation would absorb a great deal of his focus. Randy would need to put forth his greatest effort to be successful in his recovery. He was a very stubborn and strong willed young man, so he would probably bounce back quicker than most.

"Here's the last form Mr. Barker. When you sign this one, you can go get your car and pull it around to the front entrance. I will have Randy's nurse bring him to the front door," Dr. Hardy told them.

"Thank you for everything doctor. We appreciate the excellent care you gave Randy during his stay here," Blake expressed.

"No problem. We enjoyed him. I'm just thankful for his miraculous recovery. You guys take care of yourselves and have a safe trip home."

"Thank you doctor, I appreciate you," Randy told Dr. Hardy.

Blake was reeling with excitement about leaving the hospital behind them. He couldn't wait to get home. His son was finally going home. Hopefully, the worst was over.

"Dad, I miss Tabitha something awful. Do you think that I will ever stop hurting so badly? I have never felt this heartbroken before. I just can't explain it."

"I don't know Randy. I can't say that I know how you feel because I've never been through anything like this before. I can tell you that time will heal all wounds and will make it easier to deal with. It will probably always hurt when you take a stroll down memory lane. You will never get over it, but you will learn how to accept it and move on."

"I don't like to talk to Mom about any of this. It makes her too sad, and she starts to cry. I may need to speak to you from time to time about this, especially when it starts to get me down. I hope you don't mind, Dad."

"Of course I don't mind son, I love you and will always be here for you no matter what you need. I am very glad to be taking you home today; there were many times during this ordeal that I wasn't so sure you would ever be going home. I love you Randy and I'm glad you're okay. Don't ever hesitate to come to me, when you need to."

"Thank you, Dad, that means a lot to me. I love you too. I will be back to normal before long and you and I can go fishing or something."

"That sounds good to me son."

As Blake and Randy approached their home they could see quite a few cars around the house. They didn't know why, but would know soon enough. The neighbors got together and built a ramp off of the front porch to allow

Randy's easy access in and out of the house in his wheelchair.

Blake pulled up to the ramp and he parked the car. He got out and removed the wheelchair from the trunk and went to the passenger side to help Randy. Randy was in the chair and on his way up the ramp in no time. When they reached the front door and opened it, they were startled by loud shouts of "Surprise."

"Welcome home sweetheart! I love you! I hope you aren't mad at me for getting this together, but I wanted you to know how happy I am that you're finally home. I thought it might be nice for you to see some of your friends too," Jessica explained.

"It's okay Mom, I love it! Thank you very much. It's a nice surprise."

All of the kids gathered around Randy to welcome him home. They hadn't seen him since this whole thing happened and they missed him a great deal.

"Everyone come this way. We have hamburgers and hot dogs that we cooked on the grill and they're hot and fresh, so everyone dig in!" Jessica yelled.

Megan and Tara invited Tricia to the party, and Randy noticed her immediately. She was very pretty and he wondered who she was.

"Randy this is Tricia, her family just bought the Sealy's house. She goes to the high school. She's seventeen and a senior," Tara said.

"Tricia I'm Randy, very nice to meet you. I hope you have a good time."

Tricia thought Randy was very handsome. He seemed to be a really nice guy too. Maybe he would ask her out some time. She hoped so.

After a few hours of celebration, Randy got tired and left to take a nap. Everyone decided to leave and let him rest except Megan and Tara who were staying to help Mrs. Barker clean up the mess left behind.

Just as Jessica finished cleaning up in the kitchen she was distracted by a dragging sound coming from the hall. Blake had gone to the store and Randy was asleep in his bedroom; what was that strange sound? Jessica decided to go and investigate.

When she reached the hallway she couldn't believe what she was seeing. It was Randy and he was walking on his own. She was mesmerized. She was overcome by a feeling of amazement.

"Oh my God, look at you. You're walking! You're walking on your own! You're doing it Randy!" Jessica shouted.

She was flabbergasted. Her son was walking. Randy was really walking down the hall with no help at all. She knew Randy would be able to walk again, she just didn't expect to see it so soon. She was always aware of her son's strong will and determination but just didn't understand how strong it was.

"Can you believe it, Mom? I walked all the way down the hallway alone. I will be back to myself in no time at all, you watch and see. Nothing will slow me down, I mean it, nothing."

Jessica was convinced that her son meant what he was saying. He was wasting no time trying to make it happen either.

Blake had just returned from the store. He was absolutely blown over by what he saw. This is the first time he had the privilege of seeing Randy walk since his accident. He was entirely amazed.

"Randy, I don't believe it. You're standing and walking alone. How far did you walk?"

"I walked all the way down the hall, Dad. Isn't this great? I told you that I would be back to myself before long. Look at me, I'm well on my way don't you think?"

The Barkers were overwhelmed by their son's progress. He continued to get closer and closer to where he was before the incident at the fair. He was a courageous young man to say the very least.

The Thornton's were trying their best to have a successful pregnancy. They couldn't fathom the thought of losing another child. They were already grieving for Judy and didn't feel they could survive another loss. They hoped they would never have to live through something like that ever again.

Carmen Martin was still staying with Daniel and Rosy so she could spare her daughter the worry of the everyday chores. Rosy was instructed to get bed rest and intended to follow the doctor's orders to the letter. So far, there were no more episodes of bleeding. She had a doctor's appointment yesterday and he assured her everything was going great with the new baby.

"How are you feeling today, Rosy?" Carmen asked.

"I'm feeling fine, Mom. The baby is moving all over the place. She's getting stronger and stronger and she's very active too."

"Do you want me to fix you a sandwich or something to drink?"

"No, not right now, I'm fine."

Daniel finally arrived home from work.

"Hello ladies I'm home! How are you doing? I feel wonderful! I feel completely great."

Rosy noticed that Daniel was acting strangely. She wasn't sure but he appeared to be drunk.

"Daniel, have you been drinking?" Rosy asked.

"Yeah, so what if I have? I'm a grown man and I can drink anytime I feel like it. You're not my mother."

"You're right, I'm not your mother but I am pregnant with your child. Have you forgotten that?" Rosy shouted.

"I know you're pregnant. I also know that Judy would still be alive if you had been watching her like you should have. You just left her standing alone; that's why she is dead."

"I can't believe you just said that to me. Is that how you really feel? You think it's my fault Judy is dead? If that's the way you truly feel then why haven't you already told me so?"

"I'm sorry Rosy, I didn't mean it! I'm so sorry! I know it isn't your fault. Please forgive me. I love you! I'm sorry!"

Daniel walked over to the sofa and embraced her tightly. He couldn't believe what he just said. He never meant to say those things to his wife. He knew Rosy was having a hard time accepting Judy's death already. Rosy was hurt and she pushed him away.

"How could you be so mean and insensitive? I've already been blaming myself. Don't you think I know it's my fault our daughter is dead? I know I should have been holding her hand; if I would have she would still be alive. I know I killed her Daniel! I just didn't realize you agreed with me. I guess now I know."

Rosy was devastated at the words Daniel said. He was blaming her for Judy's death. She knew he had begun to pull away, but she didn't know this was the reason. She thought it was because he was having problems coping with their daughter's death, but now she realized he blamed her.

"Rosy I am so sorry. I didn't mean to say those awful things to you. I blame myself more than anyone. If I was with you at the fair that night I could have helped you with her, but I just stayed home and watched that stupid ball game. I am so sorry! I should have been there with you!"

"Daniel, it wasn't your fault. You had no way of knowing what was going to happen to Judy and neither did I. If I knew that ride was going off of the track and kill our daughter I would never have let go of her hand. I didn't know; I wish that I had but I didn't."

Daniel grabbed his wife and put his arms around her very tightly. They cried together in an attempt to release some of their bottled up frustration and anguish. They blamed themselves and they needed reassurance from each other that it wasn't their fault.

Megan and James made plans to go to the drive-in tonight. Megan's mother didn't have to work the night shift so she gave her permission to go. They weren't even sure what movie was playing but they weren't planning on watching the movie anyway. Megan decided to call James and find out what time he wanted to leave.

"What time do you want to head out for the movie tonight?" Megan asked.

"I thought it would be a good idea if we left around six or so. What do you think?"

"That's fine with me. I'll see you then. I love you!"

"I love you too. I'll see you in a while."

Chapter Seventeen

$\mathcal{I}$t was December and the days were brisk and cold. This was the coldest winter anyone could remember for quite a few years. It was slow setting in, but once it arrived it was making its mark.

Rosy Thornton was approaching her due date and so far everything was going great. The baby was very hyper and strong and never being still. She was constantly moving and playing. She could deliver any day now and was anxiously anticipating little Samantha Marie's arrival. She was looking forward to being a mother again. She missed Judy something fierce but couldn't wait to hold the new baby in her arms and look into her face. Samantha could never take Judy's place but it would lighten the burden Daniel and Rosy felt for Judy's loss.

Carmen was in the wash room folding some clothes when she heard Rosy yell. She sounded like she was in pain. Carmen ran into the living room where Rosy was lying on the sofa.

"Mom my water just broke, I need to go to the hospital. Please call Daniel; he's out in the shop working on the car. Please hurry, Mom," Rosy urged.

Carmen ran out the door as fast as she could, calling for Daniel as she ran. He heard her shouting and it frightened him. He thought something might be wrong with Rosy.

"What's wrong Carmen?" Daniel asked.

"It's Rosy, she just went into labor. Her water broke. We need to get her to the hospital."

"Okay, you get her bags and I will get the car. I'll come in after her as soon as I get the car pulled close to the door!"

Carmen ran back into the house to get her daughter's bags and set them out on the front porch. That way Daniel could just get Rosy into the car and wouldn't have to bother with them allowing them to get to the hospital faster.

Daniel was travelling as fast as he could manage and still be able to keep the car on the road. He and Rosy were scared but they were also excited. The baby was on her way and by this time tomorrow they would be parents again. They would be holding Samantha in their arms God willing and everything going well with the delivery.

Carmen was in the back seat with her trying to help ease her contractions. Rosy took Lamaze classes but right now she was hurting so badly she couldn't remember to breathe. Even though the pain was excruciating, Rosy welcomed it because the harder the labor pains were the closer Samantha was to being born. In no time Daniel and Rosy would be holding their little girl in their arms, and they were so happy.

"Breathe Rosy, breathe! You have to remember to breathe; it will make your contractions hurt less. We'll have this baby girl in no time, she's almost here," Carmen encouraged her daughter.

"It hurts Mom. I'm trying to breathe, but it hurts bad," Rosy responded.

"I know it does dear but try your best. Samantha is ready to come out and meet her family and she's in a hurry too," Carmen told her.

The hospital finally came into view. Daniel was in a hurry to get his wife to the emergency room and into the care of the doctors. He knew he didn't have the ability to deliver a baby and he didn't want to be forced into it. When they arrived he ran in screaming for the nurse.

"Help me please, my wife is in the car and she's in labor! I need someone to come and get her. The contractions are coming quickly and hard now. Her water broke about thirty minutes ago."

The nurse took a wheelchair so she could wheel her into the emergency room. But she suddenly realized Rosy couldn't stand up. The baby's head was already in view. She needed to get a doctor immediately to assist in delivering the baby. She ran back inside and told another nurse to get a doctor. Just as she turned to run back out the door she spotted Dr. Smith. She grabbed him by the arm and explained to him what was going on as they ran to the car.

"Okay little lady, I'm going to help you. We're about to have a baby here. Just breathe and try to relax. What is your name?" Dr. Smith asked.

"My name is Rosy; please get this baby out doctor. It hurts so badly!" Rosy shouted.

"Okay Rosy, I need you to push on the count of three. One, two, three, push Rosy, push!"

Rosy gave a very hard push, and the baby was out. The doctor was holding her in his arms. He didn't even have to bother to slap her bottom because she was already screaming to the top of her lungs. He handed her to her mother. One glimpse of the baby and Rosy and Daniel started to cry. She was so beautiful. She looked just like Judy did when she was born. They were extremely happy and relieved.

"Hey you, I'm your Mommy and this is your Daddy. Your name is Samantha Marie Thornton. You are so beautiful. I love you, little girl. You were born on your big sister's birthday. You would have loved her and she would have loved you, too," Rosy told her new daughter.

Daniel didn't realize it was Judy's birthday. She would have been six today. He took Samantha and just stared at her. He couldn't believe the resemblance between her and Judy. He took his little girl and he placed her on his chest kissing her on the forehead and pulling her close to him.

Samantha didn't realize the love that surrounded her. She was so sweet and innocent. Her mother and her father loved her more than she would ever know.

"Okay you two, we need to get this little girl inside and have her examined. We need to get you in and examine you too Rosy," the doctor told them.

The nurse left and returned with a stretcher to put Rosy on, and they took her inside. Today was one of the happiest days in the Thornton's lives. It was also one of the saddest days they had ever known. It was six years ago today when they gave birth to Judy and this was the first birthday since she died. This day was definitely filled with a lot of mixed emotions.

Carmen left to go with Rosy, so Daniel decided to call his mom on his cell and let her know that she was a new grandma.

"Mom it's me Daniel. Guess what?"

"What?" Jenny asked.

"You are officially a new grandma. Rosy just had the baby. Samantha is here, Mom. She looks just like Judy. She is so beautiful. She's tiny. We don't know how much she weighs yet. Rosy didn't even make it inside the hospital to have her and the doctor came to the car to deliver her. Her head was already coming out when we got here. I'm so happy. You have to see her."

"I'll come over there now. Congratulations, son. I'm glad that she is here and healthy. I will see you in about thirty minutes. I'm on my way. I love you."

"Okay Mom, I'll see you in a few minutes. I love you. Be careful."

Jenny was very excited to hear of her granddaughter's arrival. She couldn't wait to meet her. She couldn't wait to hold her in her arms and tell her that she loved her.

Tricia and Randy were the hottest new item around town. Randy completely regained the use of his legs. It was as if he had never even been involved in an accident. He was already back playing football. He still had a hard time dealing with the death of Tabitha, but he knew she was gone and he needed to get on with his life.

Tricia wasn't threatened at all by Randy's love for Tabitha. They often talked about things involving the accident and how Randy felt about her. Tricia was impressed with the love Randy felt for Tabitha and hoped maybe he would one day care for her in the same way.

Megan and James were still getting along great, but things were soon to change when James was faced with the fact that his girlfriend missed her period. Megan was three weeks late for her menstrual period. She hadn't told James yet because she was scared how he would react. She tried to warn him this might happen but he wouldn't listen to her. He had to have it his way, and now their greatest fear was about to be realized. How was Megan going to tell him she was pregnant? She would wait until she took a home pregnancy test first. If it came out positive, she wouldn't have a choice but confront him with it.

Megan already purchased the test set and decided to take it first thing in the morning. She was hoping maybe something else was the reason for missing her period. She was terrified. How were she and James going to raise a child? It was the end of December already and James only had five months remaining until he left for West Georgia College. This would definitely change their plans.

Megan cried herself to sleep that night. She was so scared and worried. She couldn't imagine being a mom as young as she was, but it was too late now. If she was pregnant, she would have no other choice but to deal with it no matter how hard it turned out to be. She was hoping she would be able to finish school, but since a baby was such a huge responsibility she wasn't sure she would have the privilege. What was she going to do?

The night left Megan tired and restless. She couldn't sleep much because she was so overwhelmed at the thought of becoming a mother. As soon as she woke up the first place she headed for was her bathroom. She hid the pregnancy test in the space around the hot water tank. She knew that her mom would never find it there.

She removed the test and followed the directions. This was the longest five minutes she ever spent in her life. When the ding went off on the timer it startled her. She was scared to even look at the results but knew she had to.

She slowly picked up the test stick off of the counter and looked in its window to see the results. She was horrified by the reading. Megan was pregnant. She dropped down onto the commode lid and burst out crying. The confirmation of her fears was unbearably petrifying. How were she and James going to do this? They were too young to be parents. How was she going to tell her mom? How were Angela and Dave going to view them now? What was Tara going to think of her? Would she abandon their friendship or would she stand by her?

She had no choice but to call James and give him the news. She dreaded his reaction.

"James, it's me Megan. I need to talk to you. It's very important. Can we get together after school?"

"Yeah, you can ride home with me if you want to. I love you. Is everything okay?"

"I'll explain it to you this evening. I love you," Megan said.

She knew she couldn't tell James before school because it would be hard for him to get through the day knowing she was pregnant. It was bad enough that she knew, but there was no sense in both of them struggling.

◦⁄ Chapter Eighteen ◦◦

ara spotted Megan walking to her locker. She seemed to be avoiding her for some unknown reason. Tara knew something was bothering Megan even though she hadn't said what it was. She decided she would just come right out and ask her if there was something that she could do to help her. She tried to wait for Megan to come to her, but obviously it wasn't going to happen.

"Megan, what's bothering you today? Is there something I can do to help you?" Tara asked.

"Nothing's bothering me. Why?" Megan responded.

"I know something is bothering you, why won't you talk to me? Does it have to do with James; did you guys have a fight?"

"No we didn't have a fight. I just don't feel too well today. I must be getting a virus or something. I'll feel better later maybe."

"Okay, but if you change your mind you can let me know; I'll be here for you. Are you going to practice today?" Tara asked.

"I would rather go home and lie down if it's all the same with you. I think I will feel better if I do that."

Tara wasn't able to get anything out of Megan. She knew something was bothering her but she just wasn't willing to share it. Whatever it was she was adamant about keeping silent.

Megan knew Tara was just trying to help her, but there was nothing she could do for her. She and James would need to work this one out together. She knew eventually her problem would be known, but she definitely couldn't tell Tara, or at least not before she told James. He had to be the first to know before anyone else could find out.

The day continued to drag on with Megan anxiously awaiting its end. She wasn't doing a good job of acting as if nothing was wrong. So far, Tara was the only one who noticed. She was avoiding James all day too. She hoped he remembered she was going to ride home with him after school. She decided she would send him a text as a reminder.

This was the longest day Megan ever experienced in her life but it finally came to an end. She left her last class early to beat the crowd out to the parking lot. She waited for James at his car so they could leave as soon as he got there.

Megan waited about fifteen minutes and finally she saw James coming. She was ready to clear the air. She didn't know how he was going to react, but was glad James would be able to help her carry the load. The burden of her pregnancy was too heavy for her to carry on her own.

"Hey, I'm glad you're out here. Let's go. I've been waiting on you for about fifteen minutes. I'm tired of standing," Megan said.

"Okay, don't be in such a hurry. Let me find my keys. What's wrong with you today? I haven't seen you all day."

Megan and James had a special spot, where they always went to make out; it was a hill that overlooked Felton. No one else knew about the place, except for their very close friends.

The drive was rather quiet. Megan kept contemplating over and over how she would break the news to James. She knew he was going to freak out no matter how she told him.

James drove the bumpy road to the top of the hill and parked in their usual place. He turned to Megan and kissed her. He attempted to make out with her, but she abruptly put a stop to it. She was in no mood for sex. That's what got them into this mess to begin with.

"James stop it! I need to talk to you about something very important."

"What is wrong with you Megan? You're acting very strange."

"You'll understand why when I tell you what's going on."

"What is it Megan? Stop beating around the bush and spit it out. Tell me!" he demanded.

"I'm pregnant James! I was afraid this was going to happen. What are we going to do now?"

"How did you get pregnant? Did you take your birth control pills like you were supposed to?"

Megan could tell right away what this was leading to. James was attempting to shift all of the blame to her but she wouldn't allow it. She tried to weigh their options but James wouldn't hear it. She knew it wasn't entirely his fault, but it definitely wasn't all hers either.

"Oh, no you don't. I won't let you blame this on me. You are just as much to blame for this as I am. I will not take the blame for it! Don't even try it James! We have to figure out what we are going to do about this. That's what we have to do."

"I think we should go to Atlanta and find a clinic so we can get rid of it. That's what I think we should do. We are too young to be parents. I start school in a few months. I don't have time for this Megan; I've worked too hard to get where I am and I'm not willing to give it up for some baby I don't even want," James told her.

"Are you kidding me James? Is that the way you really feel? I won't have an abortion, so you can forget about that. I will raise this baby on my own first. I guess you just need to take me home. I need to talk to my mother and tell her I am pregnant. I'm telling everyone that it's yours. I'm not going to lie for you. I mean it James, take me home!" Megan demanded.

Megan began to cry uncontrollably. She couldn't believe James was being so insensitive and unfeeling about this. She loved him but apparently he didn't feel the same way about her. He was only thinking of himself and his plans. She did not believe in, nor would she ever consider an abortion.

"We are not going to have this baby Megan; I mean it. You're not going to ruin our lives this way. This is crazy. We are going to Atlanta and we are going to get an abortion so no one will ever know. That's what we are going to do," James insisted.

"No we're not. I told you that I won't do it and you can't make me. I'm walking home if you won't take me," Megan told him.

Megan grabbed the door handle attempting to get out of the car but James pulled her back inside. He would not allow her to go home and tell anyone about the pregnancy. He put his hands around her throat with so much force she started to choke. She tried to fight him. She was flailing around with hands and feet flying everywhere. Megan was trying her best to get away. She scratched his face but it didn't seem to faze him. He continued to apply pressure to her throat.

The life was slowly fading from Megan. She was barely able to fight anymore. James didn't let go of her until she no longer moved. He had strangled her to death. When he realized he killed her and there was no hope for her, he started thinking how he could cover it up. He had to hide the body where no one could find it.

James got out of his car and opened the trunk. He kept a shovel there for emergencies. He removed it and went back to the front of his car. He hoped he would be able to conceal the body before anyone came by. He picked up Megan's body and carried her into the woods to bury her.

He traveled probably a half mile or so into the woods He laid Megan down and began to dig a hole. After about an hour or so, he finally managed to dig a hole, deep enough to put her body into. He threw her into the hole and filled it up with dirt. He then covered her grave with some brush and limbs. He was sure no one would ever find her. He returned to his car and started home. He was shaking all over.

When James pulled into his drive he noticed everyone was home. He went straight to his room without talking to anyone. His clothes were dirty which would look suspicious so he went straight to his bathroom got undressed and took a shower. He aggressively rubbed himself with soap as if he thought he could wash away the wrong he just committed.

When James finished he felt a burning on his face. He looked in the mirror and noticed several deep scratches from Megan fighting him and trying to fend him off. He needed to make up a story to explain his injuries.

Kinsley Keys was starting to worry about her daughter. She called her cell phone many times with no answer. Megan told her mother she was going to ride home with James. She promised she would be home early and that's why Kinsley was somewhat puzzled when she realized James' car was home, but Megan wasn't.

James had just dressed when there was a knock at his door. It was his mother.

"Kinsley just called. She wanted to know where Megan was. I told her she wasn't with you because you were already home, but she said Megan was supposed to be riding home with you after school. Did she ride with you?" Angela asked.

"She rode with me to the Busy Bee but we got into an argument, and she wouldn't get back in the car. She said she was calling Kinsley to come and get her. Didn't she call her?"

"Apparently not or she wouldn't be calling us searching for her. What did you have an argument about?" Angela questioned.

"Megan wanted to go to the movies tonight and I wanted to go hang with Tank. I told her we would go to the movies tomorrow night but it didn't seem to satisfy her."

"Will you go back and see if you can find her? What happened to your face?"

"I was riding four wheelers with Tank and a tree limb hit me in the face. It got me good too. I'll go back to the store and see if she is anywhere around there. Tell Kinsley I'll let her know something as soon as I can."

"Okay I will. Thank you. Call me and let me know too."

James went outside to his car and got in. He obviously knew where Megan was but he needed to make it appear that he didn't. He went to the Busy Bee and he went inside to ask the store manager if they saw Megan hanging around earlier.

"Excuse me, I left someone here earlier. She never made it home and her mom is worried about her. Have you seen anyone hanging around outside?" James asked the young woman behind the counter.

"No, I haven't seen anyone hanging around outside today. What does she look like?" the young girl asked.

"I have a picture of her in my pocket; let me show it to you."

The girl looked at the picture but it didn't look familiar to her. She assured him that she would contact him if she saw her. She asked for his number so she could get in touch with him if Megan did show up.

"Thank you very much," James replied.

James called Kinsley to tell her Megan wasn't at the Busy Bee. He dreaded talking to her, but he had to cover his tracks as much as possible.

"Ms. Keys, this is James. I went to the store and checked with the cashier. She said she hadn't seen her. I showed her a picture so she would know what she looked like if she came back. I also left my number so she could call me if she did see her," James told her.

"Which direction did she go when you dropped her off?" Kinsley asked.

"I honestly didn't pay attention ma'am; we had just gotten into an argument and I was angry," James said.

"What did you argue about?" Kinsley asked.

"Megan was mad at me because I decided to spend the afternoon at Tank's house and she wanted me to go to the movies with her. She was very angry when she couldn't persuade me to change my mind. She insisted I let her out of the car and leave her alone. She assured me she was going to call you. I just assumed she would," James explained.

"I haven't talked to her since early this morning before she left for school. She seemed to be bothered by something but didn't share it with me. I hope she shows up soon. If you hear from her will you let me know?" Kinsley requested.

"Yes ma'am I sure will. If I hear from her I'll tell her to call you immediately. Will you call me if you hear from her first?" James asked.

"I sure will. Thank you James. I'll talk to you later."

James felt as if he had cleverly eluded Megan's mom. He had hopefully covered every angle he needed too. He had entirely too much going for him to go down for this. He would be the last one anyone would suspect.

Kinsley Keys was extremely worried about her daughter. This just wasn't like her. She hadn't answered her phone in hours; where could she be? Kinsley decided to report her daughter missing. She placed a call to the Buchanan Police department.

"911, may I help you, please?" the operator asked.

"I need to report my daughter missing. She didn't come home after school and she's not answering her phone. I'm worried about her. This is not like her," Kinsley said.

"How old is your daughter ma'am?"

"She's sixteen. Her name is Megan. My name is Kinsley Keys. I live at 7200 highway twenty-seven, in Felton."

"I'll send an officer out to talk to you right away, ma'am."

The police were dispatched to Kinsley's house and she gave them a description of Megan and a picture. They assured her they would start a search for her daughter immediately. They promised her they would keep her updated. They gave her a number where she could call for any information concerning her daughter's case. She thanked them for their cooperation.

It had only been two months since the small community of Felton put two of their young people to rest. It was very unlikely they were ready to deal with another burden like this so soon after the roller coaster incident.

✐ Chapter Nineteen ✐

Kinsley Keys was up and down all night long. She continually checked Megan's bedroom hoping that maybe she just came in and went to bed. She called her number repeatedly hoping for an answer. It never happened. Where was her daughter? Why hasn't she called or come home yet? Kinsley was petrified with fear.

Kinsley called the number the police gave her to see if they found her daughter yet.

"Hello this is Kinsley Keys. I reported my daughter missing last night and the officer gave me this number to get any new information or updates," Kinsley explained.

"Yes ma'am this is Detective Bill Bates. We haven't been able to locate your daughter yet. We are going to the school this morning to talk with some of the kids to see if anyone can tell us anything. Hopefully someone can offer us some leads in her case. I will keep you posted. Do you know who might have been the last one to see your daughter?" Detective Bates asked.

"The last one who was with her was her boyfriend James Jackson. He said he and Megan had an argument, and she got out at the Busy Bee in Buchanan. He said she told him she was going to call me, but I haven't heard anything from her. He hasn't seen or heard from her since that time either," Kinsley told him.

"We will question Mr. Jackson and see if he remembers anything else about yesterday. Maybe she gave him some indication as to where she was going."

"Please call me and let me know as soon as you find out something sir. I will go out and look for her myself today. I was afraid to leave home during the night. I was afraid she would come in and I wouldn't be here," Kinsley said.

The night passed and still no sign of Megan. Kinsley was beside herself with fear. She couldn't help but feel like something was wrong with Megan. She should have already returned home by now. Kinsley couldn't recall an argument with her that would make her leave without explanation. She decided to call Tara and see if Megan mentioned anything to her about going somewhere.

"Tara, this is Kinsley. Have you heard from Megan? She didn't come home last night and I am very worried about her."

"No ma'am, I haven't talked to her since yesterday before school ended. She left early during the last period. She said she wasn't feeling well. I knew something was bothering her but she wouldn't tell me what it was. She skipped cheerleading practice because she said she was going home to lie down to feel better. She said she thought she may be coming down with a virus or something. When I get to school I'll ask around and see if she may have talked to someone else. I'll let you know," Tara informed Kinsley.

"Thank you Tara. I appreciate your help. Please be sure to call me as soon as you know anything. Will you tell your mom to call me, dear?" Kinsley requested.

"Yes ma'am, I will tell her right now. Maybe Megan will be at school this morning."

Kinsley knew Megan and Tara were such close friends that they always told each other everything, but

Megan had mentioned nothing to her either. Something was terribly wrong here. Kinsley just couldn't understand what was going on.

Her thoughts were interrupted by the phone. She looked at the caller ID and saw the caller was Angela Jackson.

"Hello?"

"Have you heard from Megan at all?" Angela inquired.

"No, not since she left for school yesterday morning. This just isn't like her at all. I am scared to death. Where could she be Angela? I'm afraid something horrible has happened to my baby. What if she needs me? I don't even know how to get to her. We didn't have an argument or anything so I know that's not the reason for her disappearance. I don't think she is out there intentionally staying away from home. I believe something has happened to her, keeping her from being able to get home. I'm so scared. I'm absolutely going crazy. If something bad has happened to her I don't know what I will do," Kinsley expressed.

"Try to stay calm. You know how kids are sometimes, especially teens. You just never know what they might do next. We'll find her. Do you want me to come and help you look for her? I don't have to work today so I'm free for as long as you need me."

"Do you mind? I really don't want to be by myself. We can take my car, but I would like for you to drive if you will because I am too nervous. I am shaking all over. I have got to find my little girl. I have got to find her soon," Kinsley said sobbingly.

"I'll be over there in a minute. Go ahead and get your things together and we will go look for Megan. Maybe someone has seen her. I'm sure she will turn up sometime today," Angela assured her friend.

When Angela hung up the phone she was taken aback. She was extremely worried about the outcome of this. It didn't sound good at all. She was praying that Megan was okay. She couldn't help but put herself in Kinsley's place. Kinsley had already lost her parents and her husband, and God knows she might not be able to handle another such loss. Angela decided to talk to Dave before leaving.

"That was Kinsley on the phone. Megan didn't come home last night," Angela said.

"What? Where is she?" he asked.

"No one knows. It doesn't look good at all. I hope that she is fine, but it sure does seem strange. You know how Megan is towards her mother; she would never intentionally worry her this way. She knows how much Kinsley has already been through and she always lets her know her every move. I'm very worried about her. Are you working today?" Angela asked her husband.

"Yes, I have to go in at nine this morning, why?"

"Will you please call me if you hear anything about Megan and let me know, so I can put Kinsley's nerves at ease? Will you try to find something out anyway?" Angela pleaded.

"Yeah, I'll let you know something one way or another. I love you."

"Thank you, I love you too. I'll see you later. Be careful at work today," Angela said.

When Angela arrived, she could see Kinsley already waiting for her in the car. She opened the door and she got in. Kinsley was crying so hard that she could hardly catch her breath. She was shaking terribly. Angela grabbed her and hugged her tightly to comfort her. They had to find Megan. Kinsley was on the verge of a nervous breakdown and it appeared to be just around the corner.

Tara was disappointed when she got to school as Megan was nowhere to be found. Where could her best friend be? Tara was becoming extraordinarily upset herself. Kinsley was right about the fact this wasn't like Megan, because it definitely wasn't. Where could she have gone after she got out of James' car yesterday?

There were police cars arriving at the Haralson County High School campus. They were there to conduct the investigation. They were hoping someone could steer them in a positive direction about Megan's disappearance. Their prime suspect at the moment was the Jackson kid. He was the last one to see his girlfriend. She got out of his car at the store yesterday evening, and she hadn't been seen or heard from since.

Detective Bill Bates went to the principal's office and asked him to call James Jackson to the office for questioning. He was the first one he wanted to speak with. After about fifteen minutes James finally showed up.

"I'm James Jackson. You called me over the intercom. You said I was needed up here."

"Yes we did James. There is a detective here to speak with you about Megan Keys. He's in Principal Reeves' office. You can go right in," Mrs. Terry told him.

James was jittery and nervous and hoped it wasn't obvious. Why would the police come to the school to talk to him? Did they know something? He went into the principal's office. The Detective was seated in a chair across from the door. He was the first one James saw when he entered.

"James this is Detective Bates, he is here to ask you a few questions about Megan," Principal Reeves explained.

"Hello James, how are you? I'm Detective Bill Bates and I've been assigned to investigate the disappearance of Megan Keys. I understand that you were the last one to see her yesterday. Is that right?"

"Yes sir, it's my understanding that I am," James stated.

"Where was the last place you saw Megan, James?"

"Megan was supposed to ride home with me, but she insisted I let her out at the Busy Bee in Buchanan. She said she was going to call her mother to come and get her so I didn't think anything about it."

"Where did you go after you let Megan out of the car?" Detective Bates asked.

"I went to my friend Tank's house. That's why Megan was mad in the first place. She wanted to go to the movies and I wanted to spend the afternoon with my friend. If I had known this would happen, I never would have let her out of the car. I would have cancelled my plans with Tank and gone on to the movies anyway," James told him.

"Who is Tank? What is his real name?"

"His real name is Steve Thompson."

"Is he at school today James?"

"Yes sir, I believe that he is."

"Can he back up your story about being at his house yesterday?"

"Yes he can."

"That's all I need for now James. If I need anything further I will let you know. Thank you for your cooperation."

When James left the principal's office he knew he needed to call Tank and let him know that he was at his house yesterday, before the police had a chance to ask him first.

"Tank, a cop will be requesting your presence at the principal's office and he will ask you if you were with me yesterday. I was at your house. We rode four wheelers together," James told his friend.

"You weren't at my house yesterday; why do you want me to lie to the cops?" Tank asked.

"I went to Laura Johnson's house yesterday and I don't want anyone to find out. If someone finds out, then they are going to think I am awful for cheating on Megan. Will you just help me out please?" James pleaded.

"Are you sure James? I don't want to get into trouble with the police simply because you're not telling me everything."

"I swear Tank, that's all it is. Would you trust me please? Why would I lie to you? Have I ever lied to you before?"

"No I guess not. Okay, you can count on me. How do you know that they are going to even speak with me?" Tank asked.

"Because the Detective said he was going to," James answered.

It was all set. Tank agreed to back up James' story; so far, so good. Now James could rest his nerves from worrying about it. Tank thought that he was just doing his friend an innocent favor when in reality he was giving him an alibi for murder.

"I need you to call Steve Thompson up here please. I need to talk with him and see if his story is the same as his friends." Detective Bates told Principal Reeves.

"Hello Steve, my name is Detective Bill Bates. I am the Detective investigating the disappearance of Megan Keys. I understand that you know James Jackson."

"Yes sir I do. Is something wrong detective?" Tank questioned.

"James tells me he was at your house yesterday evening. Is that right, Mr. Thompson?"

"Yes sir, James came over to my house yesterday. We rode four wheelers together. Is something wrong detective? Did James do something?" Tank asked.

"Do you know Megan Keys too?"

"Yes sir, why?"

"Megan hasn't been seen or heard from since yesterday evening, and your friend James was the last one to be in her company. He says they had an argument about him going to your house and she got mad and got out of the car. We are trying to locate her. If you think of any further information that might be helpful would you be sure to contact me Steve?"

"Yes sir I sure will," Tank assured him.

"Thank you for your time Steve, you can go now."

Tank was very confused when he left the principal's office. He had no idea that Megan was missing, and he was disturbed that James talked him into lying for him. Why would he do that? Does James have something more to hide than some simple cheating issue? Tank for sure was going to call James and question him about this.

"Why did you tell me to lie for you? They are looking for Megan. Why didn't you tell me she was missing? Are you hiding something James?" Tank inquired.

"What do you think I would have to hide for God sakes? I told you why I asked you to lie for me. Do you think I want everyone to know that I cheated on my girlfriend, especially under these circumstances?"

"I reckon it would complicate matters just a bit. Okay, I'll stick to the story then," Tank said.

James hoped he was totally convincing with the lie he told Tank. He really needed him to back up his story. He was not going to freely admit any involvement in Megan's disappearance. He would never tell anyone about what he did. He couldn't even believe the mess he was in. This was not going to be easy to get out of either. He had to be very careful in covering his tracks every step of the way.

Chapter Twenty

Angela and Kinsley printed up flyers with Megan's picture and description on them. They included several contact numbers to report anything of importance. They passed them out to every business in the local area as well as hand delivering them door to door, hoping someone, somewhere, might know something and call them.

Kinsley contacted several television stations to get her daughter's disappearance as much publicity as possible. Surely someone would know something.

Police hadn't received any leads in the Keys case at all. There were no reports of any strangers seen in town or anything unusual during the time she went missing. This told the police that it might be someone who was acquainted with the young girl. She had vanished without a trace. The only thing they knew was her boyfriend was the last one to see her before her disappearance, and he had an alibi.

Megan was missing for nearly a week now and no one knew anything. Kinsley decided to take some time at home to clean up and put her house in order. She decided she would clean Megan's bedroom and bathroom first. She was clinging to the hope she would find something to point her in the right direction.

She looked through Megan's closet and every drawer in her chest. She searched her hope chest and discovered nothing of importance, or at least nothing that would tell her where her daughter was. Kinsley worked her way into the bathroom. She scrubbed everything down and then took out the trash. That's what yielded the first clue.

When Kinsley picked the trash can up to empty it she noticed a strange packet. She removed it from the garbage and she saw it was a "Clear Blue" easy pregnancy test. Kinsley dug deeper into the trash and found the stick showing the results of the test. Megan was pregnant. Kinsley was shocked. Megan never came to her mother with this, why? Could this have something to do with her disappearance? Kinsley was determined to find out.

Kinsley went back into the kitchen and picked up the phone. She wanted to call James and see if he was aware of the new information.

"James its Kinsley, I really need to discuss something with you. Can you come over right away please? It's urgent."

"Sure Kinsley, I'll be right over. I'll see you in a minute," James said.

James wondered what it was that Kinsley needed to talk to him about. Had she found something? He went over to her house immediately following the phone call. He definitely couldn't afford to raise any suspicion.

Kinsley's deep thoughts were interrupted by the knock at the door. It was James.

"What's up?" James asked.

"I need to show you something James."

When Kinsley raised her hand there was something between her fingers. James had no idea what it was.

"What is it Kinsley?"

"It's a pregnancy test, James, and it's positive. Did you know Megan was pregnant?"

"No, I didn't. Are you sure, Kinsley?" James tried to be convincing that he was surprised to learn this.

"I know what a pregnancy test looks like, James. Trust me, this is a pregnancy test and it's positive. Are you sure Megan didn't tell you anything about this?"

"I'm sure; this is the first that I've heard about it. I don't know anything about it."

"I need to call authorities and make them aware of this new discovery. Will you let yourself out please? I'll see you later," Kinsley said.

James left and realized he should have known this crap would be known sooner or later. Why didn't Megan take her trash and discard it somewhere else; it would have saved him a lot of time and trouble. He couldn't believe this. He knew what this meant too, because the police would now really be suspicious of his involvement in Megan's disappearance.

"Can I speak with Detective Bates please? This is Kinsley Keys."

"This is Detective Bates; can I help you?"

"This is Kinsley Keys. I have some new information for you about Megan. I was cleaning up her bathroom earlier and when I went to take out the trash, I found a pregnancy test in it. It showed positive. Megan was pregnant."

"This sheds some light on everything. Do you think that she would be scared to tell you about her pregnancy? Would she possibly leave to avoid confrontation with you about this?" Detective Bates asked.

"No, she wouldn't just leave. She knew she could talk to me about anything. Megan is all I have and she knows that. She would never worry me this way on purpose," Kinsley told him.

"Okay Ms. Keys. I will question her boyfriend again and see if he can shed some light on this new information. I'll keep in touch. If you find anything else please let me know. Thank you."

Detective Bates was definitely pleased with this new information. He decided to go to James' house and question him further. He had a hunch that he knew a lot more than he was saying.

Detective Bates decided to dig a little deeper into James' background. He learned that he was scheduled to go away to college in the spring on a football scholarship. A pregnancy could sure enough put a dent in those plans. If James had to take responsibility for a baby, he would at the very least need to put his plans on hold.

On his way to talk to James he was thinking that the argument they had more than likely had something to do with her being pregnant. When he arrived at the house he noted the red mustang GT belonging to James was parked in the driveway. He rang the bell and a few short moments later the door opened.

"Can I help you sir?" Tara asked.

"Evening young lady, my name is Detective Bates. I need to speak with James. Would you get him for me please?"

Angela heard the conversation at the door. The voice was unfamiliar so she went to see who it was.

"Who are you? Why do you need to speak with my son?" Angela questioned.

"My name is Detective Bates and I am the officer assigned to the Megan Keys case. I need to ask James some questions about Megan."

"Come in sir. I don't understand; why do you need to speak with James? Surely you don't think he had anything to do with her disappearance do you?" Angela questioned.

"Ma'am, I'm not accusing your son of anything. He was the last one to see Megan and I want to make sure we don't miss anything. There is some new information on the case and I wanted to know if James was aware of it."

"Okay I'll get James. Tara, go get your brother. Tell him someone is here to see him," Angela instructed her daughter.

Angela welcomed the detective into the living room and invited him to have a seat on the sofa while he waited for James.

"James, there is a detective in the living room and he wants to talk to you," Tara told her brother.

"Did he say what he wanted?" James asked.

"He says he's working on Megan's case. He said they have some new information he needs to talk to you about," Tara explained.

"Did he say what the information was?" James questioned.

"No, he just said he needed to talk to you."

James got up off of his bed and followed his sister into the family room to speak with the detective. He was almost certain he already knew what he wanted to talk to him about, and he knew his mom was going to be very upset when she found out.

"James I need to ask you a few questions," Detective Bates began.

"Okay," James said.

"Megan's mother called me a short while ago. She found something interesting when she was cleaning Megan's bathroom. There was a pregnancy test in the trash which showed a positive reading. Did Megan say anything to you about being pregnant?"

"Oh my God, she was pregnant?" James responded with surprise.

"Yes she was according to the test. You didn't know? It was your baby, wasn't it James?"

"No, sir; and she never mentioned it to me. I had no idea," James insisted.

"Are you sure this isn't the reason you and Megan were arguing on the day of her disappearance? If you know something James, you need to tell me now," the detective encouraged.

"I don't know anything. I don't know what happened to Megan. I told you everything I know," James shouted.

"Okay detective, you've asked your questions and now it's time for you to leave. I won't have you accusing my son of something that he doesn't know anything about. James doesn't know where Megan is. If he did he would tell you. He loves her and would never do anything to hurt her," Angela said

The detective knew he had worn out his welcome so he got up and he headed for the door. He was more suspicious now than ever before. He could tell by James reaction that he knew something, and he was determined to find out exactly what it was. He was sure he had found the one responsible for Megan's disappearance, and the pregnancy provided the motive.

"Dave, I need you to come home," Angela insisted.

"What's wrong?" Dave asked.

"Some detective by the name of Bates was just here. He was asking James some questions about Megan's disappearance. Megan was pregnant. Kinsley found a positive pregnancy test in her garbage. The detective seems to think it had something to do with Megan's disappearance, and he thinks James knows something about it. They think our son has some involvement in all of this," Angela explained.

"I have to go back to the station first and then I'll be right there," Dave told her.

Dave decided to look for Detective Bates at the station. He was going to get some straight answers on what he wanted with his son, and exactly where James stood in the investigation. It sounded to him as though James was a possible suspect.

Dave located Detective Bates and asked to have a word with him in private.

"I'm Dave Jackson and James Jackson is my son. What is your motive for questioning my son? Do you think he had something to do with Megan's case?" Dave asked.

"All the evidence seems to point to him. He was the last one to see Megan, and she hasn't been heard from since she supposedly got out of his car. Not to mention the fact that she was pregnant. James stated he and Megan had an argument, and maybe it was about her pregnancy and just maybe he didn't want anyone to know about it. It might stand in the way of his future plans. That's what I think," Detective Bates said.

"James didn't do this. You have the wrong person. He had nothing to do with Megan's disappearance. James loves Megan and would never hurt her. I'm telling you that you are off on this one," Dave insisted.

"I hope you're right Dave, but if you're not, you might want to prepare yourself for the worst. You know what happens in these cases, I don't have to tell you."

Dave was furious with the assumption that James did something to Megan. He refused to believe that his own son could be capable of doing something like this. He headed home to be with his family.

Chapter Twenty-One

$\mathcal{A}$ nother two weeks excruciatingly crawled by and Megan's whereabouts was still unknown. There was no new information or new leads to investigate. Where could Megan Keys be; that was the million dollar question?

Felton was breaking ground today for a new hospital. It was going to be constructed on top of a hill with a beautiful view overlooking three other counties. Since Kinsley was the healthcare manager she was expected to be in attendance for the event.

It was two p.m. and the ceremony was scheduled to take place at three. Kinsley decided to leave early so she could get acquainted with some of the people there.

When she arrived at the location, construction was well under way. The dozers were clearing the site for the official ground breaking. They were cutting down the trees and pushing away the debris.

Kinsley was there for around thirty minutes when the sound of the heavy machinery suddenly came to a halt and people started gathering around the front of one of the dozers. She decided to get a closer look not realizing the horror she was about to experience.

The authorities were called to the site to investigate the gruesome discovery. When they arrived they kept the people away from the crime scene. They didn't want any potential evidence to be contaminated while they secured the scene.

When Detective Bates arrived he realized Kinsley Keys was there. He feared the discovery had something to do with Megan. She was missing, and the operator of the dozer just uncovered a body. It was starting to decompose but the cool winter weather slowed the rate of decay and it was still recognizable as a young female.

Detective Bates could tell at first glance the body was that of a young female. He had no doubt they had just found Megan Keys. Her mother was going to be devastated by this. He needed to verify the description of the clothing her daughter was wearing on the day she went missing.

"Ms. Keys, do you remember what Megan was wearing the last morning you saw her?"

"She had on her pink Abercrombie t-shirt and a pair of jeans with holes in the front. I believe she was wearing her Rocky boots. Why?" Kinsley asked.

"I'm sorry to have to be the one to tell you this ma'am, but I believe we just found Megan's body. Someone buried her in an attempt to conceal her remains. I'm very sorry," he sympathetically expressed.

"No, you have to be mistaken. It can't be Megan. It can't be my baby! Please tell me there is some kind of misunderstanding detective! Megan can't be dead! She's my baby! She's all I have!" Kinsley told him.

Hearing the news, Kinsley became completely hysterical. She had been here all along just a short distance from home, and she was dead. Who would do this? Megan was such a young and beautiful girl; who would hurt her? She never did anything to merit this horrible wrong against her.

"What happened to her detective?" Kinsley asked.

"We won't know that ma'am until we perform an autopsy. I promise you that we will find out what happened to Megan, and I promise you that we will find out who did it. I'm very sorry."

"Will you call me as soon as you know?" Kinsley asked.

"Yes ma'am, I will definitely call you as soon as I know anything. Please feel free to call me anytime you feel the need to. You have my number."

"Thank you, Detective Bates. I have to get out of here. I can't stay here any longer. I have to go home. I will be expecting to hear from you soon," Kinsley told him.

"If I need to know anything else I will call you. Be careful travelling home," he cautioned.

❧

Kinsley needed to call Angela and tell her that they found Megan.

"They found Megan, Angela. She's dead! My baby is dead! Someone buried her in the woods up on the hill where the hospital is being built. Megan is never coming home! How am I supposed to go on without her? She's my life!" Kinsley expressed.

"Oh my God Kinsley, do they know for sure that it was Megan?" Angela asked.

"Yes, it's definitely her. She was wearing her pink t-shirt and her jeans with the holes in the front of them. There's no mistaking it, it's Megan and she's dead," Kinsley sobbed.

"Where are you Kinsley?" Angela asked.

"I'm on my way home. I couldn't stay out there any longer. I couldn't stand it."

"Let me know when you get home and I will come over and sit with you and keep you company. I'll see you shortly. Be careful," Angela told her friend.

Angela in disbelief hung up the phone. She couldn't believe Megan was dead. How could someone kill her and then bury her that way? She knew she had to tell Tara and James before someone else did. Felton was a small community and this kind of news traveled fast. Angela called her children to the family room to break the tragic news.

"I have some bad news for you guys," Angela started.

"What is it, Mom?"

"They found Megan a short while ago?" Angela told them.

"Where was she? Is she okay?" Tara asked her.

"No, I'm afraid she isn't okay at all."

"What's wrong with her mom? Where is she?" Tara questioned.

"She's dead. Someone killed her and buried her on top of the hill where they are building the new hospital."

"Oh my God, Megan can't be dead! She's my best friend, she has to be alright! She has to be alive, Mom!" Tara shouted in horror.

"Do they know who did it?" James inquired.

"No, they are doing an autopsy and then hopefully they will know more about what happened to her and who may have done it. They will search for any evidence of DNA," Angela answered.

"I've got to get out of here. I am going for a ride. I'll be back later," James told his mother.

James went to his car, got in and raced the engine. He was terrified. He had no idea they would find Megan's body so soon. He had to devise a plan to escape all of this. What was he going to do? It was only a matter of time until they knew he killed her.

Angela took the time to calm Tara down and then went across the street to console her grief stricken friend. Angela couldn't imagine the horror of losing one of your children, especially in such horrible circumstances.

After a couple of hours or so, Angela still hadn't heard from her son. She decided to call Tank and see if he went to his house. James usually went over there to hang when he didn't want to be at home.

"Tank this is Angela Jackson. Is James over there?"

"No ma'am, I haven't seen him today, is something wrong?" Tank asked.

"They found Megan today. She's dead. He was very upset when he left here," Angela explained.

"What? Are you serious ma'am? What happened to her?"

"They found her close by. Someone killed her and buried her body. She was on the land they cleared to build the new hospital," Angela told him.

"Oh, I know that spot. They don't know who might have done it?" Tank asked.

"They are doing an autopsy to determine the cause of death and obtain any evidence which might provide some clues as to who killed her. If you see or hear from James, will you please call me?"

"Yes ma'am, I sure will. I'll talk to you later Ms. Jackson."

Tank was severely bothered by the discovery of Megan's body. He knew Megan and James always went to that location to make out. Was this the reason James asked Tank to lie? Did he have something horrible to hide? Could he have done something to Megan? He decided he would call the detective in Megan's case and let him know that he lied to him. He couldn't bear the thought of concealing potentially important information.

Back at the crime scene everyone was ordered to clear the area. Detective Bates was going over the site with a fine tooth comb looking for evidence. He thought he already knew who killed Megan Keys, but now he had to find a way to prove it beyond a shadow of a doubt. He was determined not to leave one stone unturned.

He sent all of the evidence they gathered to the crime lab to be examined. He hoped that something would turn up quickly. This young girl's mother deserved some closure and he was surely going to give it to her. Just then his phone rang.

"Hello, this is Detective Bates.

"This is Steve Thompson. I just found out about Megan and I wanted to call you and clear up the issue of

James Jackson's being at my house on the day she disappeared," Tank told the detective.

"Go on, son," Bates prompted.

"James was not at my house on the day she went missing. He called me after he left the principal's office and begged me to tell you that. He said that he went to see Laura Johnson and he was afraid everyone would think badly of him for cheating on Megan. That's the only reason I agreed to go along with him. I am somewhat suspicious of this whole thing. I know that Megan and James always went up to the location where you found her body, to make out. A lot of us kids use that spot. I hope that James didn't hurt Megan, but I don't know. If he did do something to her, I don't want to provide him with an alibi. Megan was my friend too and I cared very much for her. I will miss her greatly. This is awful," Tank explained.

"Thank you Steve, you have been most helpful," Detective Bates said.

"I'm sorry that I lied to you sir. I didn't know it was going to turn out this badly. I'll be sure to tell the truth next time, no matter what," Tank said.

Tank Thompson had just confirmed Detective Bates' suspicions that James was the one who killed Megan Keys. Things were starting to fall into place. He needed to find James and interrogate him further. Only this time, he would have his parents bring him to the station so the interrogation could be videotaped with their permission.

"Hello, is this James?" Detective Bates asked.

"Yes it is," James answered.

"Mr. Jackson, I need you to have your parents bring you to the station. There have been some new developments in the Keys case I need to discuss with you."

"Yes sir, we'll be there shortly," James promised.

James was going home alright, but it wasn't to bring his parents with him to the station. He wasn't going to the station at all. He was planning to get some of his things and some money, and take a trip.

✤ Chapter Twenty-Two ✤

ames went home and thankfully no one was there. He assumed they were across the street with Kinsley. This was the perfect opportunity for him to sneak in and grab some of his clothes and take off. He hated to do this to his parents, but he felt he had no other choice.

He went straight to his bedroom and gathered his things together as quickly as he could. He had to get out of there before someone came home and wanted to know where he was going. He took what money he had in his room, and planned to stop at the ATM on his way out of town. He had no idea where he was going; just that he had to go somewhere far away.

Down the road, James threw his cell phone out the window. He would stop and buy a prepaid phone later. That way there would be no way for anyone to make a connection to his location and track him down. He was determined to make a successful getaway.

Dave was leaving work and decided to stop at the store on his way home. He spotted James' car in the store parking lot. He went inside and approached his son not knowing James was planning to run away.

"Hey son, what are you doing?"

"I'm getting something to drink. I am going to stay the night with Tank. I just can't deal with being home so close to Megan's house. This is too hard for me," James told him.

"Do you want to talk about it? You know that I'm here for you."

"No, I don't want to talk about it right now, it's too soon. Thanks for offering though. I love you, Dad."

"I love you too son, be careful. I'll see you tomorrow."

James knew his leaving was going to tear his family apart, but not near as much as knowing that he murdered Megan. He killed her in order to keep his future plans from being sabotaged, and now it was going to happen anyway. He would never be able to go to West Georgia on the football scholarship. He would probably be on the run from now on.

Angela made plans to stay with Kinsley for the night. She was very worried about her. She was taking Megan's death extremely hard which was perfectly understandable. Angela couldn't even begin to imagine how she would be able to get through something so horrible.

Kinsley's first night was extraordinarily hard. She could remember the way she felt when she learned of Jason's death, but it didn't compare to the pain she was feeling now. She planned to go to the funeral home tomorrow and make the arrangements for Megan's burial. She knew it would take a few days for her body to be released but wished to have the arrangements in place beforehand.

Angela rose early in the morning and Kinsley was still sleeping. She left the house as quietly as she could so she wouldn't disturb her. She went across the street to make her husband some breakfast before he left to work. She noticed that James' car was not in the drive.

"Hey honey, where's James?" Angela inquired. "His car isn't outside."

"I saw him at the store last night; he said he couldn't stand to be here so he was going to Tank's house."

"He was very upset to learn of Megan's death yesterday," Angela responded.

"He was still upset last night when I saw him. He didn't want to talk to me though; he said it was too soon. So I didn't push. He will come to me when he's ready. He just has to be able to grieve in his own way."

"How is Tara doing?" Dave asked.

"Not too well at all. You know how close she and Megan were. She is taking things extremely hard. She and Megan were like two sisters."

"I know, I knew this was going to be hard for her. She will need a great deal of time to overcome this. We will just have to be patient with her. She'll eventually be able to move on, but not in the near future. I need to shower while you fix breakfast. I have to go to work soon."

Just as he sat down to the table his phone rang.

"This is Dave," he answered.

"Dave this is Detective Bates. I requested James come to the station and talk to me last night. I told him he needed to bring you and your wife with him. He told me that he was coming, but he never made it. Is he at home?"

"No, he's not here right now. He stayed the night with one of his friends. What is this about Bill?" Dave asked him.

"Your son told me that he was at Steve Thompson's riding four wheelers on the day Megan disappeared. He said he went over there after he let Megan out of his car. His friend Tank backed up his story at the school the other day when I questioned him, but he has since recanted his story. Tank called me last night and told me that James was not at his house on the day Megan disappeared. He said James had asked him to lie for him because he went to some girl's house and didn't want anyone to find out he cheated on Megan. When Tank learned of Megan's death he thought it best if he called me and told me the truth. He didn't say James was guilty of anything, but he didn't want to provide him with the alibi that he needed if he in fact was guilty."

"Tank is the one that James went to stay with last night. I will call James and talk to him about this and I'll bring him to talk to you. I don't understand why you are so adamant about this Bill? You have already made up your mind that James is guilty. He didn't hurt Megan." Dave insisted.

Dave dialed James' number and there was no answer. He decided to try and get hold of him on Tank's house number.

"Tank this is Dave, James' father. Is he available to come to the phone?"

"James isn't here Mr. Jackson. I haven't seen him since yesterday at school."

"Okay thank you Tank. We'll see you."

Now Dave was puzzled. He couldn't understand why James didn't answer his phone or why he lied to him about where he would be last night. Maybe he was just trying to catch some time alone. God forbid he had something to do with Megan's murder. Dave loved his son, but he had been a homicide detective many years and things were starting to appear very suspicious.

"That was Tank, he said he hasn't seen James since school yesterday. I can't get an answer on James cell either. What is going on here? Something isn't right about all of this," Dave said.

"What do you mean Dave? You don't think that James had something to do with Megan's death do you?" Angela asked.

"I'm not sure what I think right now. I love James as much as you do, but something isn't right about this. It doesn't look good at all. When Detective Bates called he said James was supposed to have us come down to the police station with him last night to answer some questions but he never showed up."

"He was at Tank's riding four wheelers. That's what he and Megan were arguing about. She wanted to go to the movies and he wanted to hang out with Tank. He had a scratch on his left cheek when he came home from where a tree limb had hit him in the face," Angela told Dave.

"Are you sure, Angela?"

"Yes, I'm sure because I asked him what happened when I saw his face."

"Now I know something is wrong about all of this. James wasn't at Tank's that day. James had asked Tank to lie for him about being at his house. Tank said James hadn't been at his house at all that day. James told him he went to some girl's house and he didn't want anyone to find out he cheated on Megan; that's the reason he gave Tank to back up his lie. I don't feel good about this Angela."

"Are you sure he wasn't at Tank's?" Angela asked.

"Tank said that he wasn't. When he heard the news of Megan's death he felt that he needed to tell the truth at that point. He didn't say James had anything to do with Megan's death, but he didn't want to offer an alibi when he didn't know for sure," Dave explained.

"Maybe James did go to see another girl that day. Maybe he's telling the truth about that," Angela encouraged.

"I hope you're right Angela, otherwise our son may be in some serious trouble."

Dave decided to talk to Tank face to face and find out exactly what happened.

"Tank, wait up, I need to talk to you if you have a moment," Dave asked.

"Sure Mr. Jackson, I can spare a minute or two."

"Did James tell you the name of the girl he was going to see on the day Megan went missing?"

"Yes sir, he said that he went to see Laura Johnson. He was afraid everyone would think badly of him if they found out he cheated on Megan," Tank said.

"Do you know this girl Tank? Do you think that maybe you can talk to her and find out if James went to her house that day?"

"No problem. I'll ask her next period. We have the same class. I'll call you and let you know what she says."

"I appreciate your time and trouble. Thanks a lot Tank!" Dave expressed.

This was one way to learn if James was in fact lying and maybe had some involvement in Megan's death. If Laura Johnson confirmed his alibi it would get him off of the hook. Dave was hoping and praying that his son was telling the truth. He was literally feeling sick to his stomach over the mere thought of James taking Megan's life. She wasn't just killed; she was cruelly killed and thrown away like a piece of garbage. Could his son really be capable of such a cold and calloused act? He was hoping with every fiber of his being that James was not responsible for Megan's death.

"Hello, this is Dave.

"It's me Tank."

"Did you get a chance to speak with Laura Johnson?" Dave asked.

"That's why I am calling you. She said James has never been to her house."

"Okay thanks, Tank," Dave responded.

Dave's worst fear was about to be realized. James was not where he said he was. He lied and was now becoming more of a suspect. James had so much going for him, it was difficult for Dave to believe he would throw it all away like this? Why would he kill someone he cared very deeply for?

Dave spent the rest of the evening looking for James and once again came up with nothing. They hadn't heard a word from him. Where could he be? Dave figured that James must have taken off out of fear of being suspected of some involvement in Megan's death.

Dave called Detective Bates and left a message on his voice mail.

"I just wanted to let you know that I've looked everywhere for my son and I've had no luck in finding him. I talked with Tank myself, and Laura Johnson, the young lady that James supposedly went to visit on the day of Megan's disappearance told Tank that James has never been to her house before. I am going to continue to search for James, but you may want to issue an all-points bulletin on him as a person of interest. I'm afraid that your suspicions may turn out to be true after all. Will you keep me informed? If I find him I will let you know immediately. Thanks Bill."

Dave decided to go home long enough to let his wife and daughter know what was happening. He hated to tell them that James may very well be responsible for Megan's death but he felt at this point he had no choice. Right now

James was the primary suspect and was nowhere to be found. It seemed rather obvious he was intentionally missing.

When Dave arrived home he sat down with his wife and daughter and shared his suspicions with them.

"You guys might want to prepare yourself for some bad news concerning James' involvement in Megan's death. All evidence is pointing in his direction. I looked for him all afternoon and I didn't find him. It appears he may have taken off to avoid responsibility for his involvement. I hope I am wrong, but I'm afraid that I'm not," Dave told them.

"Are you serious dad; do you think James is the one who killed Megan? I hope you are wrong! I don't know how I will handle it if I find out that my brother killed my best friend," Tara expressed.

"I can't believe that James would do this," Angela said.

"An all-points bulletin has been issued to pick up James as a potential suspect and person of interest. We're hoping to locate him soon."

Chapter Twenty-Three

The crime lab in Atlanta finally released Megan's body which was sent to the funeral home at her mother's request. Kinsley had already made arrangements for her daughter's ceremony. She was scheduled to be buried in two days.

Kinsley was devastated thinking she now would be living the rest of her life without Megan's pleasant company. She loved her so much. She had been her only family for the last eleven years. It wasn't going to be easy to go on without her. Kinsley now had no one except her friends.

The news of James' possible involvement had come as quite a blow. Kinsley thought that James cared very deeply for Megan. Why had he killed her? Her being pregnant should not have been the determining factor. She would have helped them work things out somehow. She would have been upset, but would have gotten over it.

Detective Bates had just received the report back from the crime lab and he decided to talk with Megan's mother in person. The findings were astonishing. He didn't want to deliver this kind of news over the phone.

Kinsley was putting some dishes away when she heard a knock at the door. She went to answer it. It was Detective Bates.

"Come in detective. What brings you out here?" Kinsley asked.

"I have the report from Megan's autopsy. I wanted to come in person and talk to you about the results."

"Have a seat. Would you care for anything to drink?" Kinsley offered.

"No thank you. The report showed that Megan was in fact pregnant. She was approximately seven weeks along. The cause of her death was strangulation. There was some sort of struggle before she died. We found skin under her fingernails that we believe belong to her killer. I am expecting the DNA will probably match James Jackson. When we find him we'll get his DNA to confirm it. I knew you would want to have the latest information. I am so sorry for your loss, Kinsley."

Kinsley became hysterical at the horrible way her child died. Someone held their hands around her throat until there was no life left in her. She fought them in an attempt to get away but wasn't strong enough to stop their cruelty.

Detective Bates put his arms around Kinsley and consoled her.

"Have you heard anything about James' whereabouts?" Kinsley asked.

"No not yet, but we're hopeful that we will hear something soon."

"Will you please let me know when you do?" Kinsley asked.

"You will be the first one to get a phone call. I promise you that much. I have to get back to the station; I just wanted to personally deliver the findings to you."

"Thank you very much. You have a good day," Kinsley said.

Kinsley didn't feel much like being alone, so she called Angela to request her company. She told her that she would be right over. Angela was torn between her best friend and her son's involvement. She was worried sick about James but chances were he was involved in Megan's death. She didn't know what to feel.

There was still not a single word from James. No one knew where he was. His father spent every spare moment he could afford trying to track him down, but so far no luck. He had to surface soon. There was now a national search for him as a potential suspect and person of interest in a murder.

Things at school weren't going too well either since the kids learned that James was possibly the one who killed Megan. People were saying all kinds of nasty things to Tara. It wasn't her fault that her brother killed her friend. She hated that fact too but he was still her brother, and she loved him as much as she hated what he did.

Tara was getting ready to go to cheerleading practice when she overheard some of the kids talking about Megan's death. She was extremely displeased with the harsh things they said.

"I heard you, Jimmy. You are stupid," Tara told him.

"I didn't say anything. You don't know what you are talking about. You might want to pay closer attention next time you decide to eavesdrop on someone else's conversation," Jimmy replied.

"I wasn't eavesdropping. Maybe you need to learn how to speak in a lower tone when you're being stupid and saying horrible things about people. Why did you say it if you're scared to stand behind it? You're a coward. That's what you are!" Tara shouted.

"I'm not a coward Tara, I was just trying to spare your feelings but now I don't care if it does hurt you to hear it. I said that they should hang James up in a tree and cut his throat and when all of the blood drains out of him, they should throw him into the sewer. Are you happy you witch?" Jimmy expressed with hate and anger.

"Look, I don't like what happened to Megan either; she was my best friend, but nobody knows for sure yet if James did it or not! If he did kill Megan I think he should be punished too, but it's no better for you to wish something cruel happen to him, than it was for him to do it if he did!" Tara exclaimed.

"I guess you're right. I'm sorry. I know you didn't have anything to do with it either way. I know it's not your fault. Will you please forgive me Tara?" Jimmy pleaded.

"You're forgiven. I'm very frustrated and disgusted by this whole thing myself. I'm probably more upset than any of you. Not only did I lose my best friend, but it might turn out to be at my own brother's hands. How do you think that makes me feel? Honestly! I hate it! I miss Megan! I also miss my brother, but I know that things will never be the same between us ever again because of this! Put yourselves in my shoes for a while; my path is very rocky right now and I didn't even do anything wrong." Tara told them.

Tara broke down and burst into tears. The burden she was carrying was too much. She couldn't take it anymore.

She was shaking uncontrollably. Jimmy put his arms around her and tried to comfort her. She decided she didn't want to remain at school any longer so she let Tricia take over cheer leader practice. Tricia had been bumped up to co-captain on the squad when Megan died.

Tara went to the parking lot and sat in her car. She couldn't take any more and just let go of her emotions. She could hardly catch her breath. Why did Megan have to die? Why did James have to be the one to kill her? Megan really loved James; that's one reason why it was so hard for Tara to understand.

~

James went to Florida in an attempt to hide. He didn't know anyone who lived there so he didn't have to worry about someone seeing him and knowing his identity. He could move around freely without being discovered, or so he thought. He didn't realize the local police department had received the all-points bulletin identifying him as a potential suspect.

James spent the majority of his days wondering around taking in the sights of the city unaware of the fact that his time was running out. Someone would eventually identify him. He met a girl named Christina Shasta and they were becoming quite close.

Christina really enjoyed James' company. She recently started attending one of the local colleges so she welcomed the companionship. Her family wasn't from the area and until James showed up she spent the majority of her time alone. It was nice to have someone to talk to for a change. She just didn't realize she was keeping company with a murderer.

186

James and Christina decided to spend the day at the beach together. They took along some blankets and a cooler packed with sandwiches and drinks so they could have a picnic.

Bill and Jane Sealy had begun to feel at home in their new surroundings. Florida was nice and warm, and they spent a lot of time walking along the beach and soaking up the sun. The move had been good for them, allowing them to disassociate themselves from the events in Felton. They were still left with the horror of Tabitha's death but they were no longer constantly reminded of it.

They had been following the news on the latest tragedy striking Felton. They still spoke with the Barker's quite often and were aware of the awful fate of Megan. They were aware the police were searching for James Jackson in connection with her death.

They were stunned when they went for their usual stroll on the beach, and there was James in the company of another young girl. They didn't alert him that they saw him. They put on sunglasses and hats to conceal their identities. They immediately called the Barker's and told them they just saw James on the beach. The Barker's then called the authorities and passed on the information.

"This is Detective Bates"

"This is Blake Barker. The Sealy's just called from Florida and informed me that James Jackson is there on the beach with a girl. We've kept them updated on the situation since they are former neighbors."

"Can you get a definite location on his whereabouts, Blake?"

"Yeah, I can give you Bill's number so you can call and talk directly to him," Blake offered.

"I'd appreciate that sir. Thank you very much."

The detective took down Bill Sealy's number and location, so he could alert the local authorities and have them picked up. Knowing exactly where James was should make the task simple. Detective Bates decided to call James' father and let him know their son had been spotted and they had a known location.

"Dave, this is Detective Bates. I have some news for you about James. We just received a tip he's in Florida. The authorities are on their way to his location to pick him up now. The irony of the tip is the fact that it came from Bill Sealy. He and his wife moved to Florida and while they were walking on the beach today, they observed James with an as yet unidentified female. Imagine that! I will let you know when he gets picked up."

Dave was relieved when he heard the news. He knew his son was going to have big troubles but at least he knew he was safe. He was anticipating his return.

Bill Sealy and his wife continued to monitor James to be sure he didn't leave. He was nestled in comfortably with his new girlfriend when the police arrived and took him into custody. He was a little surprised when they approached him, although he knew why. He went with them peacefully.

The local police prepared all of the necessary paperwork and after waiving extradition James was transported back to Haralson County. He would now be available to give a sample of his DNA to see if it matched the DNA found under the fingernails of Megan.

Detective Bates called Kinsley to update her on the latest development in her daughter's case.

"Kinsley this is Detective Bates, I called to advise you that James Jackson was just arrested in Florida and is being transported back here. Hopefully we'll be able to secure a sample of his DNA to compare to the DNA found under Megan's nails. I wanted to call and let you know myself."

"Thank you so much detective, I am so relieved to hear that. Thanks again."

It was late in the morning when James Jackson arrived at the jail. Shortly after his arrival a forensics technician requested a sample of James' DNA. Knowing that eventually they would get his DNA one way or another, James voluntarily gave the sample. The authorities would soon know if James was a match. The truth was about to come out once and for all.

Chapter Twenty-Four

Today was the most dreaded day Kinsley Keys would ever have to endure. It was the day she would put her daughter to rest. She could still remember the day she buried her husband as if it was yesterday, but the pain and misery she was feeling now was worse.

Kinsley no longer had any direction to her life. Megan was her life and had been for the last eleven years. How was she to continue life without her presence? The saddest part of all was the fact that her best friend's son was probably responsible. Why did James feel it necessary to kill Megan? The one secret that he attempted to hide was now out in the open anyway, and his life was very much on hold for a long long time.

In the short span of four months the small community of Felton was gathered together to lend support to the family for another one of their youth met by tragedy. Another young girl had lost her life due to someone else's harsh cruel intentions. Until this point, the town had not dealt with this kind of situation before. Hopefully this would be the final one for many years to come.

There were so many people in attendance for the service that some of the cars had to be parked across the street in another lot. Considering the circumstances the owner gladly offered its use. Because Megan was the cheerleading co-captain she was very well-known and liked by most of the kids at school. Her outgoing and friendly personality gained her many acquaintances through her life; even though few in years the impact she made on others was exceptional.

There were many beautiful flowers; mostly red roses since they were Megan's favorite. The towns' people also contributed a large sum in donations. Megan's burial expenses were completely covered and then some. This would allow Kinsley the comfort of taking a break from work to have some time to herself and to sort things out. Her life had definitely been changed forever. She couldn't begin to think about ever being happy again.

The Sealy's returned to Felton to lend support for Kinsley in her time of despair. They knew exactly how she felt; they still had nightmares about Tabitha and her terrible fate. They knew Kinsley would struggle with this for many years to come. They couldn't tell her at what point it would start to get better because they hadn't gotten to that point themselves. They still had to take one day at a time.

Rosy and Daniel Thornton left Samantha at home with Carmen so they could attend today's sad gathering. They knew it would be hard on them, but they wouldn't feel right not going because Kinsley was there for them when they needed support. They were also very familiar with the excruciating pain she was feeling. Nothing anyone could do would ease the pain, but sometimes it made things less difficult if you were surrounded by people who cared. That's the only thing that helped them during their time of suffering and misery.

Angela, Dave, and Tara, were in the front row seated next to Kinsley. They were the only real family she had and she wanted them to be close by every step of the way. The Jacksons were extremely sympathetic to Kinsley's loss and although it wasn't their fault, they couldn't help but feel they were partly to blame for this whole thing. They felt as though they should have known something, but they never suspected this could have happened.

Tara was overcome with guilt. She wished she had never tried to persuade James to change his mind about dumping Megan. If they had remained broken up, Megan would still be alive today. She would never have become pregnant and would still be with them. Maybe she should have talked to James in the beginning when he was pressuring Megan into sleeping with him. He might have become angry that Megan told her, and he might have broken up with her, but at least Megan would still have her life.

Every facet of Tara's life that she could ever remember involved Megan in one way or another. Tara felt lost now that Megan was gone. Her heart had never ached so badly. The pain was too much to handle. Would this ever get any better? Tara was in doubt.

Everyone gathered in the chapel as closely as they could and still the doors had to remain open. Not only was the chapel overflowing but the entire funeral home was packed. They had to turn on the intercoms in every room so that everyone could be a part of Megan's service. Although this was a sad occurrence indeed it was amazing to see the extraordinary number of people who attended the young girl's final gathering to say goodbye. There was no doubt that she was loved and adored.

The ceremony began with the song, "Angels in Waiting." Emotions were flowing freely among the crowd assembled to bid Megan farewell. Tears were flowing down every face. The loss of this young and tender life was absolutely heartbreaking to witness. It was not easy to understand such a cruel and devious act against such a sweet and kind young girl.

"Today is a day of much sadness and grief. We have all come together to say goodbye to Megan Marie Keys. It's never easy to accept the loss of someone who we love and adore so much, especially under such tragic circumstances. I can't give you an explanation of why this happened. I can only tell you that God has a purpose for each and every thing that takes place in our life. For whatever reason Megan's short but much appreciated life has come to an end. We will see her again one day if we make the proper preparations for ourselves. Megan would want us to go on and live our lives to the fullest in her memory. She wouldn't want us to be encumbered by the tragedy that ended her life, but she would rather we remember the joy and happiness in which she lived each second she was given. We will always hold her dear in our hearts for as long as we are permitted to live. We all loved Megan and we will greatly miss her, especially her mother Kinsley Keys. Megan was a very important fixture in the lives of many of you. It won't be easy to go on without her but we have to find a way. Let's make Megan proud of us in the way that we keep her memory alive. God bless each and every one of you. I pray that God will grant you the courage and strength to get through this," Pastor Kenneth Harmon told them.

Immediately following the words of encouragement from the pastor the song "Temporary Home" started to play. Everyone realized Megan was gone forever and would never be coming home. Her earthly body would lie beneath the ground covered with dirt for eternity. Her life was completely over. How could this happen?

Anxiety had been building in Kinsley throughout the service. She was not willing to allow them to take Megan away and bury her. She was not prepared to say goodbye to a child she had loved so much. Megan didn't deserve to die, especially not this way. James had killed her for no reason at all. He killed her to conceal something they agreed to do together. Why didn't he just break up with her? Why did he have to take her completely away from everyone who dearly loved her? This just wasn't fair. He would go to prison for a long time for what he did to Megan, but it just didn't seem to be enough. He would still be alive while Megan's life was over. He still had a chance for a better life after he spent his time in prison. How was this fair? He should be given death for his cruel and coldhearted actions. He didn't need to kill her.

The ushers were directing everyone to the front of the chapel. It was time to take a final walk around Megan's casket. One final view of the young girl and then she would be taken to the cemetery and placed into the ground. Now it was time for Kinsley and the rest of the front row to view Megan one last time.

Tara was having an extremely hard time saying goodbye to her friend too. She couldn't imagine life without Megan being there. Nothing would ever be the same for her. Nothing would ever again be exciting if she couldn't share it with her best friend. No one could take Megan's place. Megan would always be her closest friend no matter what.

194

Tara walked up to Megan and took her by the hand. She bent down to kiss her on the cheek. She started to apologize to Megan for the cruelty of her brother James.

"I am so sorry Megan. I love you so much. I don't want to be here without you. I wish I would have known what was going to happen and I would have stopped it! I wouldn't have let James kill you! I don't know why he had to do this to you! I would have helped you Megan! We would have found a way together to get through everything! I promise you we would have! I won't ever forget you. I will always love you! You will always be my best friend! No one will ever take your place, I promise," Tara emotionally said.

She didn't know how to tell Megan goodbye. The two of them were as close as sisters and they always had been for as long as anyone could remember. Tara had a long road ahead of her trying to accept Megan's death and the fact that her brother was responsible for it.

Tara turned around and buried her face in her father's chest. He led her away from the casket and out the door of the chapel. He took her to their car and then went back inside to check on Kinsley and his wife.

Kinsley was standing over Megan crying uncontrollably. She couldn't bid her daughter farewell. Megan was all Kinsley had and she didn't want to go on without her. She wouldn't let go! She couldn't!

"Oh Megan, I love you so much baby! I promised you that I would always take care of you, but I couldn't. Look what happened to you! If I had taken care of you the way I promised you would still be here with me! You would be alive and well! Please baby, just give me one more chance, and I promise you I will get it right this time! Megan please don't leave me! I can't make it without you! You're all that I have baby, I don't want you to go! You have to stay here with me! I need you sweetie!" Kinsley pleaded with her daughter.

All of a sudden Kinsley fainted and dropped to the ground. The funeral was more than she could take. They had to take her to the hospital. She would have to go to the grave side later after she was released from the hospital. Kinsley wasn't well enough to attend the burial.

Megan's body was taken on to the cemetery and put to rest in the plot her mother had chosen. Dave and Tara remained to the end of the ceremony, while Angela went with Kinsley to the hospital wanting to be with her in her time of grief. She felt obligated to be with her especially since her son was the reason for her heartache.

Angela didn't know how to feel. She was sick to her stomach from the horrible act of James. She loved her son but she was disgusted with what he did. If only there was some way to turn back the hands of time but unfortunately there wasn't any way to do that. James committed a wrong that could never be made completely right. No matter what he did from this point on nothing could bring Megan back. She was gone forever.

Angela considered her two children, and even though one could never take the place of the other one, having one child that still depended on her confirmed her need to go on. Tara still needed her no matter what.

Though Kinsley hadn't spoken a word out loud against James and what he had done, she suddenly felt the need to voice her opinion.

"Angela, why did James have to kill Megan? She loved him so much. She was dreaming of a life with him and a family. He killed my Megan and he killed our grandchild! How could he do that? Not only did he kill them, but he buried them in a deep dark hole as if they never meant anything at all. It's as if he thought he could just erase their existence. I can't understand. I loved James too! I never would have thought him capable of something this awful!" Kinsley told Angela.

"I don't know why he did this Kinsley! I've played this whole thing over and over in my mind. I've tried to make some sense out of it but I just can't! I don't know why James would do something so horrible. I haven't talked to him yet and don't know his reasons. I do know that nothing he says is going to be good enough for me. I wish I could go back and find a way to change this, but I can't! I loved Megan very much Kinsley, you know I did. I hate that this happened to her. I will never be able to understand this as long as I live! I'm very sorry for James' cruel and coldhearted behavior. I thought that he and Megan were very much in love." Angela told her friend.

"I miss her so much, Angela. I just want to wake up from this nightmare and go back to the way things were before all of this happened. I don't know how I'm supposed to get over this. What does it mean when everyone says 'go on with your life?' Megan was my life and now she's gone. I have no reason to go on. Where do I go from here? I can't take this Angela! It's too much to deal with! I just want it to go away!"

"You will get through this Kinsley. I know that it doesn't seem like it now but you will. It will always hurt, but time will help you deal with Megan's loss. It will take a lot of time, but you will learn to cope with it I promise you. I love you Kinsley and I will always be here for you. It doesn't matter what time of day or night, all you have to do is call me. I will help you however I can. We're in this together!" Angela reassured her.

Angela put her arms around Kinsley and she hugged her closely to console her. Kinsley released her emotions holding nothing back. The more she cried the better she seemed to feel. She had finally begun to grieve her daughter's passing. This is the only way that she would ever be able to heal and get on with her life. Right now, she just felt like dying so she could be with Megan.

❧ Chapter Twenty-Five ❧

*T*he results of the DNA tests were finally returned, and the skin found under Megan's fingernails was a DNA match to James. It provided proof that he was the one she struggled with in her final minutes. There was no longer any doubt whatsoever that James Jackson was her killer. Detective Bates has not yet disclosed the results to the families.

The fact that Megan was pregnant when James killed her would be taken into consideration in determining the severity of his punishment. He could very well be charged with a double homicide. He not only took Megan's life, but also the life of his own child and then attempted to conceal it.

The Jackson's had not yet talked with James. They weren't quite sure what to say to him. No matter what he told them it couldn't offer any excuse for what he had done. There was no reason good enough to justify what he did to Megan. They all loved him but they hadn't been able to look him in the face.

Kinsley wanted to visit James to hear his explanation no matter how poor it was. She decided she needed to let him know how she felt about what he did.

The phone rang and it was Detective Bates.

"Ms. Keys, how are you?"

"I'm fine, Detective. Is there something I can help you with?"

"I wanted to notify you the DNA test is back and as we suspected it was a match for James Jackson. I'm going to talk to him and attempt to get a confession. Considering we have positive DNA evidence, I don't know what he will do. I haven't talked with him since we received the DNA confirmation but I will let you know something one way or another."

"Can I come down and see James? I need to see him face to face and ask him why he did this. I need to look him in the eye while he explains his reasoning for killing Megan. I need him to know how what he did has affected my life."

"Sure, you can come down and talk to him. What time would you like to see him?"

"If I can I would like to come down around five o'clock? Will that be okay?"

"That's fine. I'll still be here and I'll personally escort you to see him. I will be expecting you then."

Kinsley was anxious to confront James with Megan's murder. She needed to sit face to face with him looking into his eyes. She wanted him to understand the horrible wrong he committed against her and her daughter.

Kinsley arrived at the police station. No bond had been granted for James because he was determined to be a flight risk in a capital offense. She requested to see Detective Bates. The officer at the front desk already had instructions to call Detective Bates as soon as she arrived.

Detective Bates directed Kinsley to wait for him in his office until he had James brought to the visiting area where she could talk to him. The first glimpse of his face caused a rage in Kinsley, but she knew she needed to remain calm if she was going to accomplish what she came to do.

"James. Why did you do it?" Kinsley asked.

"I don't know Kinsley. I really can't tell you."

"You know why you did it James and the least you can do now is give me an explanation for killing my daughter. You didn't have to kill her James. You could have just broken up with her and stopped having anything to do with her. You took her away from all of us, and you had no right to do that! I want to know why you did it!"

"Kinsley, I tried to get her to go to Atlanta so she could get an abortion but she refused. She said she would raise the baby on her own. I knew what people would think of me if I didn't help her. I wasn't ready to be a father. I had my football scholarship and everything. It wasn't long until I would be going away to college and I didn't want anything to stand in the way. There's no way that I would have been able to go to college if we had the baby."

"You can't go to college now James, can you? Everyone knows Megan was pregnant and they also know that you killed her in an attempt to hide it. What do you think everyone thinks of you now?"

"I know how much I've screwed up. I wish I could go back and change it but I can't. I didn't mean to kill Megan! I just wanted her to agree with me. I wanted her to have the abortion. She tried to get out of the car while we were still arguing. She said she was going home to talk to you and find a way to work things out. I panicked and I grabbed her around her throat and I started to choke her. She scratched the side of my face. By the time I realized what I had done it was too late, she was already dead. I was scared someone would find her so I dug a hole and I put her body in it. I was hoping no one would find her there. I thought it would be easier for everyone if they didn't know for sure what happened to her. I'm sorry! I'm really sorry!"

"Unfortunately James, I'm sorry just isn't enough to fix this one. You killed my little girl and then you threw her in a deep, dark, cold hole like an animal. Megan was the most important thing in my life; she made every day worth living for me, and you took it all away. How could you do that James? I hope for the rest of your life, every time you close your eyes you see her and what you did to her. I hope you never find peace. I loved you James and so did Megan and you repay our love this way? How could you do that to us? You will never find anyone who will love you as much as Megan did. I hope you spend the rest of your life in prison looking over your shoulder every moment in fear of the people surrounding you. I pray you spend the remainder of your life with the same horror that Megan felt those last moments she lived. I will never forgive you for what you have done nor do I ever wish to see you again. I hope you get what you deserve during your trial and sentencing. I pray that the system gives Megan justice against you."

Kinsley put the phone down and she walked away from the window where she was talking to James. She said everything that she wanted him to hear and then quickly ended the conversation. She was not willing to accept his apology for killing Megan; it wouldn't bring her back. She would kill James herself but she knew that she would then be no better than him. She would let the justice system take its course and punish him for what he had done. She had faith that it would. With the evidence against him and the DNA match, there was no way James would escape justice.

Dave and Angela finally decided it was time for them to go and talk with their son. Tara didn't want to go. She was so overcome with anger toward her brother; she didn't even want to see him, much less talk to him. She didn't know if she and James would ever be able to mend their relationship. Her parents thought it best not to push Tara. She had a right to her feelings, and this was an extremely difficult situation to deal with, especially considering that Megan was her best friend.

When they arrived to the station they went to the visiting area. The first sight of him after all of this, held a number of mixed emotions for them. They loved James but they were so angry with him for taking Megan's life.

"James, how are you?" Dave asked his son.

"I'm fine, Dad, except for this mess I've made of things."

"Why did you kill Megan?" his mother asked.

"I don't know why, Mom; I know I made a terrible mistake."

"That's putting it very mildly James. You took that young girl's life—and for what? To hide some mistake you made, that is now out in the open anyway. Only now the mistake is much larger than it was in the beginning. We could have found a way to work it out in the beginning, but now there's no way to fix it. Megan is dead and so is your unborn child. How could you do that James? I want to know what happened that day and I want to know now!" Angela demanded.

"Megan called me that morning before school and told me she needed to get together with me to talk to me about something important. She said she would ride home with me that evening and we could talk then. I had no idea she was going to tell me she was pregnant. When we went to the top of lookout hill, I thought we were going to make out or something. That's when she told me she was pregnant." James continued to tell her the entire story. "I loved Megan, but I didn't want to be saddled with the responsibility of a child. I knew it would stand in the way of my plans for school and everything, and I didn't want to be a father yet."

When he looked back at his mother he could see the tears rolling down her cheeks. He knew how much it hurt her to hear the details of this horrible crime. He loved his mom and with the evidence against him, he knew they would have found out what he did, and strangely enough he wanted to be the one to tell them.

"James, you killed Megan because she wanted to do the right thing and take responsibility for her actions. You didn't think that maybe you could have still gone to school and the rest of us could have helped out in the situation. You killed her to conceal the pregnancy that you freely contributed to and it's out in the open anyway. Everyone knows about it and now you are known for something more terrible than that; you are known for the murder of Megan Keys. We knew Megan all of her life; you were raised together. She was your sister's best friend and you only thought of your own selfishness when you decided to take her life. Why didn't you stop and think about everyone else involved in this? You have managed to completely tear many lives apart and all for the sake of avoiding responsibility. I am so ashamed of you James. We raised you so much better than this. Megan was a human, not some stray animal that you could kill and discard, as if her life was of no importance. How could you so easily do away with a life that you said meant so much to you? It's very hard for me to accept the fact that we have raised someone with so little conscious. I don't know that I will ever be able to get passed this. I love you James, but that's about all I can say. If you weren't my son, I wouldn't even have that for you."

Angela couldn't even stand to look at James any longer. She had nothing else to say to him. She loved him, but she almost thought it would be easier to deal with his death, rather than the truth of what he had done. He created a tragedy with his own hands and he could have made the choice to spare Megan's life, but he chose to take it away.

Dave had a few things he desired to say to his son as well. He needed to make him understand that he did not condone his actions nor would he ever forget the horrible injustice that he committed against Megan Keys. He would not stand behind him or try to help him get away with what he did.

"I don't know what to say to you son. I can't believe that I sit before you today with this horrible truth hanging over us. You had no reason to take Megan's life. You could have made another choice; a smarter choice. You could have taken responsibility for what you did. Megan didn't get pregnant herself; it wasn't a choice that she made alone. She became pregnant as a result of a mutual decision the two of you made together. I have been on the right side of the law for many years now. You knew how I felt about things like this and yet you didn't care. The only thought you had was for yourself and your football scholarship. I am so disappointed in you. If Megan were my daughter, I know I would want you to pay to the full extent of the law for what you did. I hope when you have spent your time in payment for your awful deed that you are wise enough to never make a careless decision again. I love you but I will not stand behind you in this. You need to pay for what you did and that's what you are going to do." Dave said.

"I'm sorry for what I've done, Dad. I will never do something like this again, never."

"I'm sorry just isn't enough here, James. It doesn't matter how many times you say I'm sorry Megan will still be dead. There's nothing you can do to change that. I hope that you have figured out on your own how cold and malicious your actions were. Megan still lies in a grave, and her life is over because you didn't leave her a choice. I never would have thought you would ever be capable of murder and it really breaks my heart to have to accept the fact that you are."

Dave couldn't stand the heartbreak of talking to his son any further. He had committed a horrible crime and now he had to pay for what he did. James was the only one who truly knew the depth of his own heart and mind. No one but himself could know for sure how sorry he really was. Time would be the only factor in determining the truth of what James promised. He was a seventeen-year-old boy who had already found himself capable of murder. Where would the next twenty years find him?

✐ *Chapter Twenty-Six* ❧

etective Bates intended to offer James the opportunity to confess to Megan's murder. He would offer to help him get a lesser sentence if he admitted to the crime. James had already explained the horrific events of that tragic day to Kinsley and his own parents. He knew that police had his DNA match for evidence. He knew there was no way to deny his responsibility in Megan's murder and he decided he would more than likely accept a plea bargain.

"James, remember me?" Detective Bates asked.

"Yeah, I remember you detective. How can I help you?"

"It's more about the way that I can help you, James."

"Oh yeah, and just what can you do to help me? No one can help me now. It's too late for help!" James shouted.

"No, it's not too late. If you agree to record and sign a confession, I can make things somewhat easier on you. I will ask the prosecutor to drop the death penalty in exchange for life in prison. But the only way I will ask is if you agree to a confession. You know the evidence we have against you and you know you're going to be found guilty either way, but your confession will prevent a long drawn out jury trial. We can go before the court and explain your remorse as evidenced by your voluntary confession and cooperation and hope for a reduced sentence."

"I may as well go ahead and give you my confession. There is no way to get off of these charges. Everything is stacked against me. Set it up and I will give you what you want," James agreed.

Detective Bates arranged for James to provide a recorded and signed confession. James knew he was going to prison no matter what but at least this way he would avoid the death penalty. He didn't want to die even though he hadn't given Megan the same opportunity.

Kinsley was glad that James would finally pay for what he did to Megan, but she felt he shouldn't have been given an opportunity for a lesser sentence. Megan never got a choice, so did he really deserve one? She didn't think so. Many times she pictured herself standing face to face with James and a gun in her hand. In each instance she easily pulled the trigger with no regrets. She didn't want to tarnish Megan's memory in that way. Megan would never have approved of handling this situation in that manner.

Kinsley went to Megan's grave every day. She had to be near her even if it was only to be close to her body. It was extremely hard to sit at her grave and talk to her with the silence of no response. Kinsley missed her daughter so much. Megan was buried in the plot next to her father's grave. Now she was with her father who had never been privileged enough to meet her in life. She had her for sixteen years and she loved her very much, but now Megan would spend eternity in the presence of her father. Kinsley imagined a happy reunion between the two.

Tara's life was immensely altered too. She constantly felt as though there was emptiness inside her that she just couldn't rise above no matter how hard she tried. Tara and Megan had always done everything together, and now that

Megan was gone there was less excitement in everything she did. Eventually she hoped to once again find happiness in her future but right now it just seemed to be far away in the distance.

Tricia and Tara became close friends but Tricia could never take Megan's place. Megan would always have her own special spot in Tara's heart regardless of who crossed her path. Tara felt as if she had lost her sister. She would never forget Megan and the happiness of knowing her.

Tara still hadn't gone to see James. She didn't feel like she would ever forgive him. He had no right to take something that meant so much to everyone, away from them. Tara loved James but she didn't ever want to have anything to do with him again. As far as she was concerned, he was dead also.

Angela and Dave had a difficult time dealing with what James did. They loved Megan as if she was one of their own children. It would be many years until they would be able to have anything to do with him. They had to grieve first, and then they had to try to heal. They weren't sure that complete healing was possible; but maybe they would eventually reach a place—where James was concerned—that it might be possible to exchange letters with him.

The Jackson's had to be certain their son was truly sorry for what he did before they would ever consider contact with him at all. The son they had loved and nurtured for seventeen years had taken the life of a young girl simply to hide his own mistake. His only thought was for himself and his own desires.

The court accepted James' confession and guilty plea to the murder of Megan and her unborn child. In consideration of his cooperation, he was not given the death penalty. The judge did, however, feel the vicious and cold-hearted manner in which he committed the murders made him a danger to society. He handed down a life sentence without the possibility of parole. The remainder of seventeen-year-old James Jackson's life would be spent in prison.

The small community pressed forward with the memory of the "Felton Tragedies." In four short months they had been faced with three murders and one near death. They dearly hoped and prayed this terrible fate would never find them again.

✐ About the Author ✎

$\mathcal{M}$ y love and passion for writing was apparent very early in my life. I started out with an admiration for poetry. It always amazed me that individual words with little meaning, when placed together, could create tremendous emotion. I have never been able to express myself well verbally; but with the written word, I can speak from my heart.

When I was younger—and even as an adult—it became a habit to write a personal expression of poetry for my parents on holidays in place of a store-bought card. It meant so much to me as I watched tears flow from my mother's eyes as she read the words. This told me she found the sincerity of my warmth and love in the words I so carefully wrote. My father's eyes would light up and he would hug me and tell me how special it was to him that I gave him something from my heart. My parents were always supportive of my talent with words, giving me tons of encouragement along the way. I'm extremely thankful to them.

I have two daughters, a wonderful husband, and a much adored granddaughter who means the world to me. I have three stepsons, one stepdaughter, and five stepgrandchildren whom I love and adore. My life has been filled with much excitement along the way. I've experienced every emotion life has to offer, but most of my memories are filled with joy and happiness. I've truly been blessed.

The simple things in life are very pleasing and relaxing for me. Things like sitting on the front porch taking in God's beauty and delight, and listening to the wonderful sounds of nature.

My favorite hobbies include writing, of course, sewing, reading, and working in the yard. I am very thankful for all of the blessings that God has placed in my life, and all of the wonderful things he has allowed me to be a part of. I definitely know—with no uncertainty—who guides me in my journey through life.

I believe the most important things in life are God, family, love, and closeness. I was always reminded that as long as these things were present in my life, I had much to be thankful for.

I would like to express a special thank you to Brighton Publishing for the confidence they placed in my work. "Thank you, from the bottom of my heart."